THE LIFE OF TERRY BROOKE

Lorenzo CARVELLI &
Alessandro INCALZA

CONTENTS

"A FEW WORDS BEFORE WE BEGIN..."

Amid this profound silence, a remarkable realization strikes me: I am on a sacred journey, embracing confessions that surpass the ordinary. Especially as we approach the final leg of the human voyage—that pivotal moment when fiction loses its grip and raw, unfiltered truth emerges. It is then that sincerity bares itself, shedding layers of deceit as a futile attempt to evade the inevitable. However, it's crucial to note that I will cloak myself in anonymity to safeguard those who confide in my humble self. Names will remain shrouded, and while the stories are genuine, they may be transformed—not to obscure the truth, but to preserve my sacred oath of confidentiality. However, this pledge does not demand that the shadows of these unspeakable sins fade into oblivion with me. I am a confidant who has been entrusted with a confession.

Signed: A priest.

THE GAME

THIS STORY, BURIED like many others, began in a desert—in the desert of Texas, to be precise... in a place where probably no one has set foot since. The endless desolation spanned under an orange dawn. The horizon was dominated by a vast cloudless sky as the sun rose, illuminating the rocks and sands.

An ancient truck clanged along a dusty road, its tires kicking up swirls of sand as it ventured into the wilderness. Shortly, it lurched to a stop, disgorging a young man and woman in their late teens, their determination palpable despite the weariness etched into their dark features. Each wore simple, weather-beaten clothes and a small backpack. They were two desperate immigrants, like so many others.

The young man approached the driver, a burly man with auburn hair and black eyes. They exchanged a few sharp words before the driver pointed decisively northward.

As the truck faded into the distance, the young couple, bound by an unspoken bond, set off into the desert's embrace.

Hours later, under cover of night, a small fire flickered amidst some ancient ruins, casting dancing shadows upon the weathered stones. The boy and girl were huddled together for warmth.

"Está haciendo mucho frío," the boy remarked, his breath forming mist in the chilly air.

The girl responded with a soft smile, and they sat in contemplative silence, surrounded by the vastness of the desert night.

Unbeknownst to them, Todd Branson, a solid man of twenty-seven, was watching in the distance. He emanated a predatory aura as he peered through his binoculars, his black Stetson aiding his camouflage.

His voice sliced through the stillness with a chilling edge. "Gentlemen, I think I found some scum," he declared, his words dripping with malice.

Turning to his accomplices in the truck, Todd's gaze fixed on Andrew Williams, a trembling figure whose apparent innocence and fear belied the darkness within.

"You alright, Andrew?" Todd asked, his tone carrying a veiled threat. Andrew nodded nervously, his fear palpable. "Yeah."

Sensing Andrew's trepedation, Todd's lips curled into a cruel smile. "Can ya feel the adrenaline pumpin' through yer veins?" he sneered, his eyes glinting with sadistic pleasure. Andrew nodded, his compliance born out of sheer terror. "Good. From now on, yer a part a' this," Todd declared. Andrew nodded again like a puppet in Todd's twisted game.

With a sinister tap on the vehicle's roof, Todd signaled to the driver, Richard Heydrich, to start the engine. "Let's hunt."

Everybody was ready.

Richard sat next to Barney Brown. The two of them could have been brothers along with Todd, all three sporting dark hair and beards, suntanned skin, and athletic builds. They had been nothing but schoolyard bullies just a few years before. Now, they were utterly lost in sin.

As they sped towards their unsuspecting prey, Barney callously discarded a liquor bottle. The sound of breaking glass echoed through the night, with no one else to hear it.

Under the desert's watchful gaze, the two young travelers slumbered beside their dwindling fire, enveloped in a fragile cocoon of false security.

Suddenly, the roar of a powerful engine pierced the night, jolting the boy awake. With a sense of foreboding, he watched Richard's pickup truck materialize from the darkness, its lights switched off.

As the girl stirred from her sleep, fear spread across her face. The pickup began its predatory dance around the desert ruin, sealing the couple's fate with each menacing revolution.

With a screech of tires, the truck stopped. Todd emerged, jumping from the back, his weapon drawn and his intentions clear.

"Get out! Get the fuck out!" His voice cut through the night air like a blade.

Huddled together in terror, the couple stepped forward, powerless against the encroaching darkness. Barney and Richard joined Todd, their malevolent presence casting another shadow over the scene. Todd advanced towards the trembling girl, a sadistic grin playing on his lips. "Stay right there!" he barked, his command laced with menace. Meanwhile, the boy, paralyzed by fear, found himself held in place by the barrel of Barney's shotgun.

Turning to Andrew, Todd issued another command, his tone dripping with malice. "Andrew, go get the crowbar from the truck," he ordered, sending the lanky blonde youth on a journey into the darkness. He fumbled through contents of the truck bed, grateful for an excuse to hide his face.

Under the oppressive night sky, Richard and Barney tackled the girl to the ground, their vile intentions evident in their leering gazes.

"Y'all got no idea what's comin' for ya!" Richard taunted with sadistic mirth.

"Let's see them tits!" Barney jeered, revealing the girl's anguish.

"Please, no! ¡No me toque!" the girl pleaded, her cries falling on deaf ears as their hands began tearing her clothes off and hitting her with repeated slaps.

Andrew returned with the crowbar in hand, uncertainty etched on his face. Realizing what was happening, he turned to Todd, stunned. "What's goin' on? This is wrong."

"It ain't wrong, Andrew. It's revenge. So, are you with us or against us?"

A long silence followed as Andrew stared at the object in his hands. "What should I do?" His voice trembled with apprehension, his moral compass wavering in the face of Todd's malevolence.

Seizing the younger man by the shoulders, Todd directed his attention towards the other captive, his words dripping with venom. "Look at 'im, Andrew! This scum comes to our country uninvited. They ain't got no respect for no permits and they steal our jobs," He hissed, poisoning Andrew's mind with hatred and prejudice. Andrew and the boy locked eyes, Todd's words hanging heavily between them.

"Think of all the sacrifices yer parents made, and how they died on a measly pension. Think about the fact that now yer findin' yourself sweepin' floors for one of 'em!"

Todd's insidious whispers echoed in Andrew's ears, clouding his judgment with bitterness and resentment. With a tightening grip on the crowbar, Andrew hesitated, torn between morality and bitterness.

"What're you waitin' for?" Todd's whispered. The command rang in Andrew's ears like a sinister mantra, pushing him forward toward the brink of depravity.

"¡Por favor, no!" the boy pleaded desperately, his voice choked with fear.

Andrew raised the crowbar in a moment of brutal clarity, his resolution crystallizing into action. The sound of metal meeting bone echoed through the night, followed by the boy's anguished screams blending with Richard and Barney's laughter. As the boy's cries faded into silence, suffocated by tears, Todd's twisted grin displayed his satisfaction. His depravity knew no bounds as he forced himself upon the girl, her struggles a futile attempt to escape his vile grasp.

"Stop it!" Todd commanded as the girl's screams pierced the darkness.

"Please, no! No!" she pleaded, desperate for mercy.

"Fuck! Stop it!" Todd's frustration boiled over as he wrestled with his victim. In a moment of defiance, the girl managed to scratch his face, eliciting a howl of pain from her assailant.

Undeterred, Todd retaliated, his violence escalating as he pinned her hand to the soil with one of his own. "Just wait one second, little Missy..." He took a knife hidden under his jacket and drove it through her hand, pinning it to the ground. She shrieked, but her assailant merely laughed. As Todd's depraved act reached its sickening climax, Richard eagerly awaited his turn, his anticipation palpable.

"Hurry up, man!" Barney's impatience betrayed his eagerness as Richard took Todd's place.

"All right, Barney... don't push me!" Richard's retort was laced with a hint of malice as he positioned himself above his helpless victim.

Having exhausted all their indecency, Todd, Richard, and Barney stood amidst the desolation, their shadows dancing in the fire's flickering light.

As they shared a moment of contemplation and cigarettes, Andrew's haunted gaze betrayed the trauma of the atrocities witnessed.

"Andrew, check their backpacks! See if they got wallets," Todd ordered. Amidst the girl's anguished cries, Andrew rummaged through her belongings, his hands trembling with unease.

"Get anything?" Todd's inquiry cut through the night air, his curiosity tinged with cruel indifference.

"No. Just water and sandwiches". Meanwhile, he found an old book inside the bag, of which he only glimpsed the author's name: Terry Brooke.

Barney approached the boy, his revolver drawn, offering one last look of indifference from a face smeared with blood. A single gunshot echoed through the night, marking the end of the boy's suffering.

As the first light of dawn crept over the horizon, the girl, battered and broken, watched as the sun rose on a new day, her tears giving way to a solemn acceptance of her fate.

For her, the nightmare was about to be over.

Across the desert landscape, the sunrise painted the canvas of the sky with vibrant colors.

Barney sifted through CDs within the pickup truck while Todd lit up a joint and sighed, his senses absorbed by the tranquility of nature.

The digging of a small pit nearby marked Richard's next dark intentions.

In her final moments, the girl's whispered prayer resonated amidst the desolation, a plea for divine intervention in the face of unspeakable horror.

"The whore's still alive!" Richard's callous remark was met with calm reassurance from Todd, his eyes closed in contemplation. He murmured with a sense of finality, "Not for long."

Andrew stood amidst the carnage, draped in a blanket. His green gaze was fixed upon the rising sun as he grappled with the darkness within and tried to find solace in nature's beauty.

With a deceptive tenderness, Todd lay beside the dying girl, his whispered words a cruel mockery of affection. "Shhh. It's almost over, mi amor," he cooed, his touch a macabre caress against her battered form. Swiftly, he retrieved the dagger from the girl's hand, where it had been stuck all night long. His actions were imbued with ritualistic solemnity. He stood and extended his arms towards the heavens, enacting a grotesque parody of reverence, before driving the blade into her chest.

In her last fleeting moments, as her eyes fluttered open for the final time, her gaze was locked on Todd's as he grinned. Then, with a final exhalation, her eyes shut, and she succumbed to the embrace of darkness.

THE STRAINS OF Janis Joplin's "Move Over" echoed through the desert, the radio signal distorted and yet somehow clear for a few seconds amidst the vast sand and sky.

A vibrant van traversed the arid landscape, adorned with psychedelic swirls and laden with musical instruments. Laughter and music filled the air as it rumbled along the desert road, carrying within it the hopes and dreams of its passengers.

Daly was seated in the passenger seat, a slender woman in her mid-twenties, with a spirit as wild as the desert wind and her wavy chestnut hair. Her voice joined the chorus of the radio, her passion for music evident in every note she sang.

With her were the members of her band: Dylan, the drummer, whose steady rhythm anchored their sound; Mark, the guitar man, whose fingers danced across the strings with effortless grace; and Nina, the driver, band composer, and manager, whose wisdom belied her age.

Despite the uncertainties of the road, their spirits were high, because they were on tour.

Daly, the heart and soul of the band, poured her emotions into the lyrics of one of her all-time favorite songs. Her voice, tinged with longing and raw emotion, resonated through the van, sending shivers down the spine of anyone who listened. As her bandmates seamlessly joined in, their voices merged in perfect harmony. It was as if the very desert itself was alive with the sound of their music.

"The experience was truly electrifying, you know? It felt like stumbling upon an incredibly talented artist, a rare flower in bloom. Those who had the privilege of hearing her sing were completely captivated; she was like a being one could only admire—a celestial presence gracing the earth—and there was no other way to perceive her. All one could do was earnestly hope that she would receive every bit of goodness the world offered".

"Yeah. Tell me why we're playing out in the middle of nowhere," Dylan asked, riffing off the lyrics. Dylan's inquiry interrupted the somber melody, prompting laughter and jests from the group. Their banter filled the van, mingling with the rhythmic tapping of drumsticks against the front seat.

"Marfa is where I was born and raised, and I'm lookin' to take a leap," Daly confided with a hint of melancholy.

Nina offered words of encouragement: "Don't worry, Daly. Even though Marfa wasn't a planned stop, we're happy to make it! After all, it's the alien city, or something, right?!"

The two boys exchanged glances and decided to simply share a silent sigh. With renewed resolve, Daly gazed out at the passing scenery, her eyes filled with the desert and the anticipation for the city ahead.

Each passing mile brought them closer to Marfa, a beacon of hope shimmering on the desert horizon.

A few minutes later, right inside the city, the van came to a stop in front of a bar. Daly emerged with a smile, her eyes shining.

"Home Sweet Home!" she declared, feeling a sense of belonging.

With renewed purpose, the band members gathered their instruments and equipment. The dimly lit bar pulsated with energy as Daly and her band made their entrance, instruments in hand. The singer's eyes scanned the crowded room, landing on Andrew, who was diligently cleaning the space. Recognition flickered across her face as she approached him, a surprised smile lighting up her features.

"Andrew!" The young man's mop halted mid-swipe as he turned to face Daly. Genuine warmth was evident in her greeting. "How are you?"

"Fine! You?" Andrew's response was buoyant, his mood visibly lifted by Daly's presence.

Glancing towards the rest of the band, he inquired, "You here to play some tunes?"

"Of course!" Daly's response was filled with enthusiasm, her anticipation palpable. The arrival of the bar owner, a Hispanic man who exuded authority, interrupted their conversation.

"Hey there, cowboy! That darn floor ain't cleaned up yet, and I want to see myself in it. Claro?" The bar owner's command was delivered. With a whispered promise to catch up later, Daly gave Andrew's arm an affectionate squeeze before turning her attention back to the bar owner. "What're y'all standin' 'round fer? Git a move on!" The bar owner's directive was met with swift action from the band and they headed toward the stage.

Andrew watched from the sidelines, his gaze following Daly's every move. She turned back just for a sunny smile, for him.

A few hours later she was there, on the stage, looking undeniably sexy with her tight jeans and unbound hair.

The opening chords of "Piece of My Heart" filled the air, Daly's voice soaring above the crowd as the performance began. She commanded the stage with her mesmerizing presence, her swaying hips and sultry voice captivating the audience as she delivered a soulful rendition of Janis Joplin's classic. She drew the audience into her world of passion and longing, each note infused with raw emotion. The venue pulsated with energy.

Unnoticed by the young star, Todd watched intently before disappearing into the throng.

Andrew stood mesmerized, his gaze fixed upon his childhood friend as she poured her heart and soul into the music. In that moment, he was enchanted by her presence, captivated by the magic of her voice.

After the gig, in the dressing room…

Daly removed her makeup as well-wishers passed by to congratulate her. Although she was completely sweaty and exhausted, her happiness was palpable. People came in and out of the dressing room to offer quick hellos and once alone…

Daly blushed and grinned at her reflection in the mirror. With a playful flourish, she scrawled her signature in lipstick onto the glass, only to be interrupted by Andrew's reflected appearance.

"Hey, Daly!" Andrew's greeting was met with genuine affection as Daly rose to hug him.

"God, I missed you, sugar bear! How are you?" Daly's warmth enveloped Andrew as they embraced.

"I'm doin' just fine, thanks for askin'. How 'bout yourself?"

"Heck yeah, I'm still playin'! There's nothin' better than livin' a rock 'n roll lifestyle, am I right? I'm workin' on a record too! Are you still playin'?"

Daly's enthusiasm was infectious, and he was smiling, even as he said, "No, since my grandma passed… I gotta think 'bout my own needs and ain't got no time to mess 'round." Andrew's tone was tinged with sadness as he reflected on his circumstances.

"I feel you. Sorry 'bout your grandma, she was a good 'un. I know what it's like to grow up solo." Daly's empathy shone through as she offered her condolences.

A knock on the door interrupted their conversation, and Daly and Andrew turned to see Todd entering.

"What's good, Daly? You back home yet, Rock Star?" Todd's presence elicited discomfort from Daly, but she responded politely. "Alight, just here for tonight." She was eager to change the subject— or the room.

Another group of random fans leaned into the room to offer congratulations before departing, leaving Daly to smile gratefully.

She took the opportunity to quickly excuse herself, citing the need to huddle up with the band, leaving the two guys in a long silence.

"She's still the head honcho just like she was back in school, ain't she?" Todd's observation hung in the air as Andrew, at a loss for words, continued to stare after the singer. Not getting a response, Todd decided to leave Andrew alone with his thoughts.

In the dimly lit backstage corridor, Todd strolled along, pausing abruptly to take a swig from his flask. Behind him, Richard and Barney approached, both appearing high.

"Buddy! We been lookin' for you!" Richard was filled with excitement as they caught up.

"Where you been at, man?" Barney chimed-in, showing a small, colorful pill on his tongue.

Todd grabbed his friends by the collars, speaking in a low, urgent tone. "Fellas, I was stalkin' my prey."

"Here?" Richard's disbelief was apparent as Todd nodded.

"Yes. My prey is here." The leader's eyes narrowed as he revealed his intentions to his companions. Richard and Barney exchanged surprised glances, the gravity of his words sinking in.

Richard started hesitantly, "But... Bob says—"

"I don't give a fuck about Bob. Y'all gotta help me out!" Todd's urgency was evident.

"How?"

Todd laid out his scheme. "Y'all gotta take Andrew for a ride, get 'im high too, and then roll with me. I need him to attract my prey. Give 'im some of them pills!"

"Who's the prey?"

"Daly Flores."

"Daly Flores? The prom queen, huh?" Richard's recognition added a layer of intrigue to Todd's plan.

"You got it!"

After showering and preparing to leave, Daly took a moment to indulge in a cigarette near her van. The desert night enveloped her, the stars casting a dim glow over the vast expanse. Unbeknownst to her, an ominous figure approached stealthily, moving like a shadow in the night.

"Boom!" Nina startled Daly, sending her hands down her spine to tickle her. She enjoyed a hearty laugh at the singer's expense, but Daly's initial fright soon morphed into annoyance.

"Hey, sorry sis! Won't do it again! You look spooked, though."

Daly reassured her. "No, I'm fine. The gig got me pumped!"

"Hell yeah! That was great!" Nina's admiration was evident as she enveloped her in a hug.

"Have you seen Andrew?"

"Andrew who?" Nina's response was casual, her attention already drifting elsewhere.

"The boy... Ah, forget it! Never mind!" Daly quickly dismissed the thought of Andrew, redirecting her attention to her bandmate.

Nina pulled Daly into another hug, affectionately kissing her on the cheek. "Anyways Sis, talkin' seriously, I think I picked up a local dude. He's waitin' for me in the parking lot... He's got somethin' to show me if you wanna come along."

"Alright, alright! I got the picture." Daly's response was dismissive as she brushed off Nina's invitation.

"If you change your mind, you know where to find me! Love you, Sis!"

"Love you too".

Nina walked away, leaving Daly to contemplate her next move.

Just before disappearing into the night, Nina turned back, her gaze locking with her friend's. "Daly... I love you. And I will protect you forever!" With those heartfelt words, Nina took one last sip from her drink and vanished into the darkness.

Meanwhile, from inside a car parked nearby, a pair of eyes observed Daly as she continued to smoke.

THE END OF A DREAM

IT WAS NIGHT and in the serene tranquility of Marfa's streets, Daly meandered through the maze of her thoughts, accompanied only by the soft shuffle of her footsteps on the deserted asphalt.

The dim glow of streetlights cast playful shadows on her face, while the night breeze gently tousled her hair. A sense of melancholy enveloped her soul, the weight of intertwined memories clinging to the familiar streets. Suddenly, the sound of an engine broke through, interrupting the flow of her thoughts. Daly turned to see a dilapidated car slowly approaching.

"Hey, Singer!" the voice startled her, although she immediately recognized it, and the face, illuminated by the glare of the headlights.

"Todd?" she responded, caution lacing her tone.

"Yo, it's me. You ghosted me without a word, but it's cool. You up for a cold one or what?"

Todd's casual invitation caught Daly off guard. She eyed the budget beer in his car with a hint of amusement.

"Uhm... Splurgin', huh?" Daly quipped, a playful smile dancing on her lips.

"Oh, check this out..." Todd delved into his bag, producing a plastic pouch filled with marijuana.

"This here's 'Sour Diesel'. Wanna chill for a minute? For old times' sake..."

Daly's playful facade cracked ever so slightly, a flicker of curiosity shining through. Her mind briefly revisited their school days, where Todd was once merely a bully. Now, as an adult, he exuded an aura of easy friendliness... or so it seemed. His invitation stirred in her a sense of intrigue, tempting her.

"Alright then, let's get a move on!" Daly's eagerness shone through as she stepped into his car with a mix of uncertainty and nostalgia. "I gotta meet up with the band later. I don't wanna be late, okay?"

"You won't," Todd assured her with a confident smile, igniting a spark of anticipation within Daly as they set off into the night.

"That night...Oh, that night..."

About half an hour later, their car stopped near a small creek. It was a desolate spot, with only darkness and silence for miles in every direction.

"We ended up in the middle of nowhere, huh?" Daly remarked. "I ain't tryin' to be a party pooper, but why'd we have to be all the way out here for a sesh?"

Todd got out of the car, saying, "Just relax a bit," then went to sit by the riverbank, leaving the car door open. After a few seconds, he lit a joint. Daly felt a bit guilty and went to join him.

By the river, the two sat together, smoking weed and drinking beer, immersed in the tranquility of the night.

"You never know who's snoopin' around in that town—better safe than sorry. And this place is just plain magnificent!" Todd remarked, gesturing to their surroundings.

"Yeah, for real, this place is fire. I almost forgot how damn beautiful it is out here," Daly concurred, appreciating the scenery as she gazed at the moonlight reflecting off the water. In the distance, the "Marfa Lights" flickered, adding something magical to the atmosphere of the night.

Suddenly, a pickup truck approached, and Daly tensed up at the sight of it.

"Somebody's comin'!" she noted with concern.

"Don't worry! It's just my boys!" Todd reassured her, his tone excited. As Richard and Barney emerged from the truck, their intoxicated state was evident. They shoved also shoved out Andrew, who appeared disoriented and unsteady on his feet.

"What's with him?" Daly was instantly concerned and went to help support him. The young man started to vomit.

"He just got his first taste of the real deal, ain't that right, boy?" Barney remarked with a smile. He was high.

"We might have given him too much..." Richard admitted with a laugh.

"I think so. Todd, we need to call an ambulance. I think he's overdosin' or somethin'!"

"Alright y'all, let's get this party started," Todd declared, signaling a shift in the atmosphere.

Richard and Barney moved to block Daly's escape route and began eyeing her with lustful looks. Barney unzipped his jeans, brandishing his manhood at the cornered girl, laughing mockingly. Daly's panic mounted as she realized the danger she was in, but before she could react, Todd struck her across the face, silencing her protests.

"Scream if you want to. Ain't nobody gonna hear you though," he warned, as he began to assault her.

"No, please! No!"

"Ya like this?"

From that moment on, everything in Daly's mind became a whirlwind of chaotic images and pain. Despite her agony, she managed to open her bloodshot eyes one last time. She heard Barney's grunts, felt Todd's menacing presence, and saw the storm clouds gathering ominously on the horizon. Cloaked in darkness, Todd prepared to document their depravity with a camera, while Andrew, confused and stoned, struggled to comprehend the new nightmare unfolding before him.

Todd was filming saying,

"Get her jacket on and fill her pockets with rocks; we'll toss her in the river before the downpour hits!" Richard was dropping the shovel and grabbing Daly's body by the legs. "Richard, slit her throat!!"

"Wait! I'm busy now!"

Daly's body was once again brutalized. Eventually, a burning sensation gripped her throat, the warmth of the blood soon turned icy on her chest, and life began to drain from her kind brown eyes. Finally she was tossed into the river.

The group of criminals drove away in the van, dragging along Andrew, who was almost dead himself.

"I don't know if you get me… She was dead! But…"

A few minutes later, amidst the relentless rain, thunder, and the tumultuous rush of water, a sudden flash of lightning revealed Daly emerging from the water. Gasping for air, she clutched her throat, coughing and choking.

Struggling, she was swept away by the unforgiving current, vanishing into the darkness.

On the same night, just a few hours later, it all began with a single siren.

Todd, Richard, and Barney chose to spend that evening in a gambling den, playing poker as if nothing were amiss.

With a cigarette dangling from his lips, Todd casually examined his cards while engaging in laid-back conversation with the other players. In the background, the sound of another approaching police siren filled the air.

Amidst the casual banter, one of the players mentioned the ongoing police activity, speculating about the reason. Seemingly unfazed, Todd suggested, "It could be a robbery," before stubbing out his cigarette.

Another player chimed in, revealing the true reason for the police sirens: "A girl was brutally assaulted near the river."

Todd's demeanor subtly shifted as he absorbed the news, exchanging a knowing glance with Richard, who appeared visibly troubled. As the player elaborated on the girl's ordeal, describing her survival against all odds, Todd's expression darkened with a mixture of anger and apprehension. Unable to articulate his emotions, he focused on the silent television news report playing on the screen behind the bar, the caption highlighting the word "survived."

In the early morning hours, under the cover of darkness, the pickup truck rumbled into the hospital parking lot, Todd at the wheel and Richard beside him. Barney watched the scene from the back, Andrew looking ill at his side. The air was thick with tension, the scene alive with onlookers, flashing cameras, and vigilant law enforcement. Squinting through the smoke of his cigarette, Todd surveyed the chaotic scene before him. Richard broke the uneasy silence, suggesting, "We gotta go in, right?"

"Oh, sure! Let's just waltz right in with all them cameras!" Todd's response dripped with malicious sarcasm, his gaze sharp with disdain as he considered Richard's proposal. In a sudden, brutal display of dominance, Todd seized Richard's hand, snuffing out his cigarette on the back of it with sadistic precision. Richard recoiled in agony, his screams drowned out by the cacophony around them.

Barney, unsettled by Todd's brutality, watched in silent discomfort, still groggy from the weed.

With a mixture of frustration and calculation, Todd scolded Richard for his recklessness, emphasizing the danger they faced. And indeed, it was crucial. In that group, the only one with a lick of sense was Todd.

Nursing his injured hand, Richard vented his anguish, demanding answers from his leader, who remained silent. Contemplating their next move, the Todd's gaze shifted toward the hospital entrance with a glimmer of determination. Recognizing the gravity of the situation, he turned to Andrew.

"Hey Andrew, you okay?" The young man's expression was one of resignation as he reluctantly nodded, his gaze lingering on the hospital with poignant sadness. Todd stared at Andrew's face for a long moment. He knew perfectly well that he was a coward after all, but he needed to keep an eye on him. With a decisive nod from Todd, the engine roared to life. "I'll talk to Bob, and we'll figure out how to put an end to this little inconvenience."

They disappeared into the night, leaving behind a hospital brimming with police officers, journalists, and curious bystanders.

"I know plenty of folks won't remember, but the news got around on a bunch of channels and folks kept up with it for a bit—just a few weeks. 'Cause when it comes down to it, who cares about the victims? Only their kin, and if you ain't got none, you're all alone. And she was just that—truly alone."

A few nights later, Daly lay in a hospital room filled with the steady hum of medical equipment. Bandages were wrapped around her neck, and bruises marred her once vibrant skin as she remained in a coma.

Outside, in the corridor, a weary police officer settled into a chair, his exhaustion evident as he stifled a yawn.

Meanwhile, Todd, disguised as a janitor, wheeled a cleaning cart down the hallway, whistling a tune. He exchanged nods with the officer before starting his fake duties.

As the predator swept the corridor, a nurse approached the officer, delivering a message about a phone call—the signal Todd had been waiting for to set his plan in motion.

With a grunt, the officer rose to answer it, leaving Todd alone to carry out his dark task.

In less than a minute, alone in Daly's room, Todd prepared a syringe with a lethal dose of morphine, addressing Daly with sinister familiarity.

But…

Todd's nefarious plans were interrupted by Andrew's sudden appearance. "Don't you dare touch her!" His voice cut through the tension of the silent night.

"Andrew?! What the hell are you doin' here!? Get out before we're caught!" Todd snapped back.

"You didn't get it, did you?! Lay a finger on her, and I'll scream!" Andrew retorted defiantly.

"Scream all you want, you idiot, and you'll end up in jail with us!" Todd countered. Andrew hesitated, intimidated, and Todd seized the opportunity to threaten him. "I've got the footage, the recordin's from that night, and if memory serves me right, you were there too! So, if you plan on sinkin' us, know that you'll sink along with us!"

"I don't care! Don't touch her!" Andrew stood his ground, determined to protect Daly at any cost, and in the end… he succeeded.

Todd checked his watch and realized he had run out of time. "Alright Andrew, you've won this round, but you know what? Watch your back, 'cause you just brought your day of reckonin' a whole lot closer!"

Todd left the hospital room, banking on the fact that Daly was, after all, in a coma, and would remain so for a while. In his mind, Andrew became the new problem—the first on the list—and he intended to deal with it as soon as possible. Andrew watched from the window as Todd exited the building. Then he watched Daly for a long moment before breaking down in tears and making his own retreat.

GOD

IN THE DAYS that followed, Todd lived with a persistent knot in his stomach. The fear of being caught at any moment gnawed at him, driving him to hole up in his house.

In the dimly lit basement, adorned with a Confederate flag, the air reverberated with the thunderous strains of metal music. Todd, shirtless and wearing a World War II soldier's helmet, exhaled a cloud of smoke from his cigarette. As he took a swig from a bottle of bourbon, his gaze fixated on his reflection in the mirror. The mirror revealed a naked young woman, one often scene around a particular street corner, reclining on the bed.

"Come on, Todd! Get over here!"

Turning towards the beckoning voice, Todd's attention was diverted by the ringing of the phone. With a swift motion, he lowered the volume of the music before answering the call in a terse tone. "Yeah?"

"The girl woke up."

Finally, it came—the announcement he'd been dreading.

Meanwhile, the prostitute's voice persisted. "Todd, come here!"

A familiar voice from the other end of the line interjected urgently. "Todd!"

Todd's mounting tension erupted as he flung the bottle against the wall, the glass shattering into a thousand shards right beside the bed. "Shut the fuck up!" he yelled with anger and fervor. Amidst his palpable distress, the prostitute recoiled in fear.

"Yah ain't got nothin' to worry about," reassured the voice on the phone. "She woke up, but she don't remember a damn thing... She's scarred for life, talkin' nonsense. I reckon the judge's gonna lock her in a loony bin and throw away the key."

A fleeting sigh of relief escaped Todd's lips. "Alright, alright. Did ya track down Andrew?"

"Not yet," came the reply, "but from what I've heard, it looks like he done hightailed it outta here real quick without sayin' nothin' to nobody."

Another sigh escaped Todd's lips, laden with frustration and uncertainty. "You still got the tape, right?" inquired the voice on the other end.

Seeking support, Todd leaned against the wall, grappling with the weight of the situation.

"Yeah, but ain't nothin' visible on that video... it was too damn dark, and the footage is useless."

There was a long pause. "Well, no harm done... He doesn't know anyways".

"And so it shall be," Todd affirmed tersely.

"Well, I reckon you're gonna carry this story for a good while... but you gotta tie up loose ends as soon as possible." He paused. "Answer me! Was I clear?"

"Clear as day, Bob," Todd replied, his tone tinged with resignation.

In some ways, Bob was superior to Todd, and Bob knew this well. Todd had made too many mistakes. He needed to be more careful. Fortunately, the other man didn't seem to want to make a big deal out of it. "Alright, I'll keep you posted if I hear anything 'bout them two. You steer clear of any more headaches!"

With a sense of begrudging acceptance, Todd stubbed out his cigarette. "Okay".

The line was cut off.

The bleakness of a gray day draped over Dallas. A heavy shroud of snowflakes drifted down lazily from the overcast sky.

A solitary bus grumbled to a halt at the curb, its doors exhaling with a soft hiss as Andrew descended, a worn bag slung over his shoulder.

With a thoughtful gaze, he surveyed the wintry landscape until his eyes alighted upon the imposing silhouette of the Dallas Theological Seminary. The crunch of snow beneath his boots echoed his inner turmoil as he approached the threshold. With a solemn creak, the heavy wooden doors swung open, beckoning him into a new chapter of his life.

TEN YEARS LATER

IT WAS SNOWING all over the city. The sky was gloomy, and even the psychiatric hospital was covered in a thick white mantel. But inside, there was the sound of joy.

A Christmas carol filled the common room, blending with the festive vibe created by the decorations festooning the space. Nurses, sporting Santa hats, bustled around, doling out treats to the patients who gave them hearty holiday greetings.

Amidst the cheerful scene was Daly, now thirty-four-years-old, seated in a wheelchair, her once lively spirit dimmed with the passage of time. Her posture was strained and a prominent scar marred her neck.

Daly observed her surroundings with a distant gaze, lost in her own thoughts. Approaching with a warm smile, Nurse Emily offered her a homemade snack. "Daly, do you want a piece of cake?"

The former singer's response, though somewhat disconnected from reality, hinted at a glimmer of her former self. "No, thanks. I'm waiting for the band to come pick me up," she murmured dreamily.

"What? What band, Daly?" As confusion flickered across Nurse Emily's face, Daly's delusion briefly faltered, offering a fleeting glimpse of the stark reality of her existence. "Daly, are you okay?"

No response. Emily was swept into a dance by another nurse.

With a heavy heart, the former singer propelled herself toward the window, her excitement tinged with a poignant longing for something that would never be.

A fellow patient, munching on cake, offered her well wishes for the new millennium, unwittingly underscoring the stark passage of time. The realization crept in slowly, Daly's anguish palpable as she confronted the harsh reality of her circumstances.

She faced the weight of years gone by… stolen.

The former singer rose from her wheelchair, silently slipping away from the laughter and chatter of the common room.

As she passed the abandoned nurses' station, she noted shadows swaying ominously, dancing with the television's flickering glow, and heard music. Daly, ensnared by the singing competition on screen, watched with a mix of fascination and yearning as a contestant captured hearts and imaginations. As the song's final notes hung in the air, the patient's eyes glittered with admiration, her dormant dreams stirred by the performer's impassioned delivery.

With a silent resolve burning in her chest, she dragged a chair beneath the open window—the one on the floor that wasn't barred. Without hesitation, with the outside world calling to her like a distant siren, Daly made her choice. She slipped through the window and into the yawning abyss below. The impact of her body against the ground echoed through the silent night.

"And here her part in the story ends… I suppose."

A few days later, many miles away, in St. Joseph's Parish in San Antonio, Andrew, now a priest, was playing his violin, filling the air with melancholy melodies.

Seated nearby him, Reverend McInney, a figure of wisdom

and compassion, listened attentively. He was tall and solid-looking, despite age and infirmity, a youthful twinkle in his blue eyes. As the music filled the room, the Reverend, ever observant, noticed the shadows that lingered in Andrew's eyes as he finished Mozart's "Requiem".

"Bravo!" McInney's enthusiasm for the music was real and palpable as he eagerly exclaimed, "You should get back to playing in the orchestra!"

"Nah, I reckon I'm done with that. Just a mere pastime now, and that's fine by me. Wasn't all that good anyways."

"Nonsense!" McInney retorted, rising to his feet with the aid of his cane. His health may not have been the best, but the old man was certainly a cherished presence for Andrew, and there was a mutual respect between them.

"Maybe playing would be a way for you to socialize again. You've been holed up too long, only seeing me. And don't get me wrong, I'm mighty fine with just your company... but I'm old! You're young and should be out havin' fun!"

"You know I'm more of a lone wolf, Reverend," Andrew replied.

"Sure do, been knowin' you for near 'bout ten years," McInney responded with a yawn, a silent understanding passing between them. As Reverend McInney bid Andrew goodnight and retreated into the quiet of the church, Andrew was left alone with his thoughts, the strains of his violin echoing once more, the sensation more eerie now for lack of an audience.

Outside the grandeur of St. Joseph's Parish, a lone figure moved with silent purpose toward the church's entrance, drawn by Andrew's music.

The man's movements were stealthy; like a thief, he entered the dark hall of the church.

Andrew's office was shrouded in darkness, save for the soft glow of the laptop screen as he diligently wrote his sermon. His fingers paused briefly to clean his glasses. The young priest eyed the bottle of whiskey, his silent companion, on the table.

Suddenly, a dark figure materialized at the door. It was Todd, his presence chilling and ominous. "Hey, Andrew." His voice dripped with malice.

Andrew was startled, fear creeping into his expression. "What're you doin' in here? What do you want, Todd?" His voice trembled.

Todd's eyes wandered to a painting of the Virgin Mary before fixing back on Andrew. "It's nice here, ain't it? Has it saved you?" His tone was taunting.

"What do you want?!" Andrew's fear was palpable.

Todd's smile was sinister as he delivered the news. "Daly's dead. She done walked out a window." Andrew gasped and muttered a prayer, visibly shaken by the revelation. "Well, I came here just in case ya had any doubts about my behavior... And I'll be damned if I ain't tempted to finish the job and wrap everything up tonight, but..." Todd gazed out the window, Andrew watching him warily.

"You see, Andrew, my life is set up real good right now. I've put a lot of things right... I got a big business on my plate, and I don't want any problems."

"What're you tryin' to say, Todd?" the priest's voice was strained.

"I just wanna make sure ya ain't got no dangerous conscience naggin' at ya, and also to make sure yer gonna protect the truth."

"Protect the truth? Funny choice a' words..."

Todd's patience wore thin as he pushed a nearby statue off its pedestal with a crash.

"Look how easy it is to break things in here! If I weren't damn sure that at least twelve cameras have already got me on video, your brains would be splattered on the floor by now!" Father McInney, praying on his knees in the chapel, heard the crash of the statue. "Damn technology... It ain't like the good ol' days. But then again... it was that same technology that helped me find ya.

"Todd, you'll pay for yer sins! You'll pay dearly!"

I feel bad for ya, but turns out I'm pretty darn smart. While you were away, I became the mayor. I got my town in the palm of my hand, and it don't turn out well for anyone who crosses me."

"I'm tellin' you, yer gonna pay, and everyone's gonna know what a sneaky, dishonest dirtbag you are!"

Todd revealed a revolver, and Andrew stepped back, intimidated.

"Look at you, coward!" Todd and Andrew locked eyes, tension thick in the air. Eventually, Todd backed down and left, issuing a chilling warning. "Don't make me come back. You won't make it out alive."

Father McInney, hidden nearby, sighed sadly before slipping away into the darkness of the hall.

Todd's footsteps echoed softly against the pavement as he retreated from the church, swallowed by the stillness of the night. He retrieved his cell phone from his pocket, while the faint sound of ringing was filling the air.

"Hey, Todd. Did ya find 'im?" The voice on the other end was Bob.

"I did," Todd responded tersely, his tone devoid of emotion.

"You know we gotta get this done, right?"

There was no urgency in that voice. It was just a fact.

"I know, I know... I'll find a way to make 'im disappear."

"Good. See you at mine when you get back."

"It'll take me five damn hours… but okay. Later!" Todd concluded, ending the call with a decisive click of the phone. As he slipped the device back into his pocket, Todd's gaze flicked uneasily to his surroundings, a sense of paranoia gripping him.

In that same minute, Andrew stepped into the dimly lit room, exhaustion etched into every line of his face.

With heavy footsteps, he made his way to the bed, sinking onto its worn surface with a sigh. His gaze drifted to the bedside table, where a solitary drawer beckoned to him. He pulled it open, revealing its contents in the soft glow of the room's single lamp. His fingers brushed against the smooth surface of an old, sealed letter, a reminder of the past. Inscribed on the old envelope were the words: "In case something happens to me". A sense of uncertainty lingered in the air.

Andrew hesitated for a moment before carefully extracting the letter from its confines. Nestled within the folds of the letter lay a photograph, yellowed with age, but still vivid in its depiction of happier times. Andrew's gaze lingered on the image of himself and Daly as children, a bittersweet smile tugging at the corners of his lips before he reverently returned it to its rightful place. With a flick of his wrist, Andrew extinguished the light on the bedside table, enveloping the room in darkness as he allowed the weight of the evening's events to settle over him.

The next day, the solemn strains of choir music filled the hallowed halls of St. Joseph's Parish as Andrew stood before the congregation, his hands steady as he administered the sacred host. Suddenly, the doors of the church swung open, in the middle of the mass, casting a shaft of light across the church. Andrew's gaze faltered, a flicker of unease crossing his face. A figure emerged from the light of the outside; her presence was like a disruption to the sanctity of the moment. She was Terry Brooke, clad in sleek black attire and shielded by dark sunglasses, who took her seat with an air of quiet determination. Her arrival went unnoticed by the congregation, but it deeply unsettled Andrew, who had been interrupted while blessing the body of Christ.

Despite the intrusion, Andrew continued the Mass, his voice steady despite the turmoil brewing within him. Yet as he raised the sacred host aloft, his thoughts strayed to darker places. None of the parishioners seemed to notice, but Andrew had felt the woman's gaze upon him from the moment she had entered the church. He vaguely knew her, or rather, he knew her name even though he couldn't remember why. Regardless of her attractiveness, the presence of that woman was somehow extremely burdensome. Andrew decided not to dwell on it too much and proceeded with his Mass, ardently wishing to be alone as soon as possible.

The same night, alone in the dimly lit sanctuary, Andrew sought solace in the embrace of the crucifix. Its silent presence was shrouded in the darkness. With trembling hands, he lifted a bottle of whiskey to his lips; the burn of the liquor was a welcome distraction from the pain that gnawed at his soul. Clutching the photograph with Daly to his chest, Andrew allowed himself a moment of vulnerability. With each swallow of whiskey, he sought refuge from the demons that haunted him. The bitter taste of regret lingered on his tongue.

As the night wore on, Andrew sought sanctuary within the confessional. The darkness offered a fleeting respite from the chaos of the world outside. But his solitude was short-lived, interrupted by the unexpected sound of footsteps, high heels clicking on the floor. It was Terry Brooke.

Her presence was a jarring intrusion on his dangerous solitude.

"Forgive me, Father, for I have sinned," Terry's voice pierced the silence.

"Who's there? Oh, it's you," Andrew responded.

"I'm a newcomer around these parts, Father. I don't feel welcome. There's envy, resentment, hypocrisy, and vengeance festering within me. And… my thoughts are so impure, Father!" Terry confessed.

Andrew was visibly annoyed by the woman's intrusive presence, but after all, he was a priest, and it was his duty to provide comfort, even reluctantly and at such a late hour.

"God won't punish you for your thoughts. Is there more?"

She nodded and then began to speak. Andrew listened with a heavy heart as Terry poured out her sins. Her words echoed hauntingly his inner turmoil. She was, after all, a troubled soul like all the others... but even as he offered absolution, a sense of unease lingered. The weight of his guilt pressed down upon him like a suffocating shroud.

As Terry departed, her footsteps echoed through the empty church and Andrew was left alone once more, grappling with the ghosts of his past.

As he returned to the solace of his whiskey, he knew that the shadows that haunted him would not be so easily banished. It was time to stop them. The effect of the alcohol was kicking in, but perhaps it wasn't enough.

That night, numbing himself wouldn't be enough, and he knew it well. He was just buying time, like the coward he had always been.

Andrew stumbled into his room, his movements unsteady, and his mind clouded by the haze of despair. With a heavy heart, he collapsed onto the bed, the weight of his burdens pressing down upon him like a suffocating blanket.

Tears streamed down his cheeks unchecked, his sobs echoing through the empty room. In a fit of frustration, Andrew struck the nightstand. The blow brought a wave of helpless anger, and he threw his laptop to the floor in a desperate attempt to silence the relentless onslaught of his thoughts. His hands shook as he reached for another bottle of whiskey.

Shortly after, in the heart of the night, Andrew found himself drawn to the solitary solace of the church tower. He didn't know how he got there; his feet had simply moved on their own… showing him that it was time to end it all.

He couldn't go on anymore.

On that rooftop, the distant city lights shimmered in the darkness below. Clutching the whiskey bottle tightly in his hand, he leaned against the railing, his gaze fixed on the dark horizon as tears blurred his vision. The wind whispered through the night, carrying with it the echoes of distant sirens and the faint rustle of leaves. Andrew's heart ached with longing as he cried out into the void, his voice a desperate plea for absolution. "Please! Help me! Talk to me, Father! Show yourself, God!"

With trembling hands, Andrew stepped closer to the edge, the yawning chasm below beckoning to him like a siren's song. The bitter taste of whiskey lingered on his lips as he closed his eyes, his mind consumed by thoughts of the life he had lost. But as the darkness closed in around him, a sudden sound shattered the silence, wrenching Andrew from the brink of oblivion. His eyes flew open in terror as he whirled around to face an unexpected intruder, his heart pounding in his chest. A terrifying and strangely familiar voice spoke. "You're not capable, you see; even to commit suicide takes a minimum of courage that you don't have… But I'll help you… to die."

Andrew's eyes widened, sensing his end was near. Something attacked him, and there was no time to defend himself; it was just time to fall.

Father McInney found himself shouldering all the burdens and responsibilities that come when someone leaves his life. In the stark light of day, Father McInney sat in the sterile confines of the police station waiting room, his features etched with sorrow. Beside him, a drunk homeless man slumbered in a chair, oblivious to the world around him.

Father McInney sighed wearily, his thoughts drifting to the events that had led him to this place, his heart heavy with the burden of guilt and regret. As a policeman approached, Father McInney rose to his feet, his cane clutched tightly in his hand. With a heavy heart, he followed the officer into the sterile corridors of the police station.

The encounter with the police was brief. Few details were exchanged, and many doubts were left hanging. It was hardly a surprise; Andrew's soul had always been tormented more than usual due to his sensitivity and some lingering guilt.

That same afternoon, in the subdued light of Andrew's room, Father McInney packed away photographs and belongings into boxes. He paused momentarily, holding a photo in his hands, his expression heavy with sorrow. With a sigh, he set it aside and continued his task.

With each item packed away, a sense of finality settled over the room—a silent acknowledgment that Andrew was gone forever.

A FEW YEARS LATER

YEARS LATER, UNDER the scorching desert sun, two vans rumbled along the dusty road, leaving billowing clouds of dust in their wake. Todd, now aged and heavier at forty-five, led the procession in the first van, while Barney, similarly aged and significantly heavier, followed with another one.

Inside Todd's van, a subtle shift in the cargo caught his attention. Meanwhile, Barney's voice crackled through the walkie-talkie on the dashboard. "Hey Todd, I was wondering'... Why ain't Richard with us?"

"Some of his boys quit on him," Todd replied gruffly, "and he's gotta stay back at the office". A few shocks reverberated against the van's body, and Todd held a curse between his lips.

"Did they find out he was scammin' 'em?" Barney inquired.

"Probably," Todd responded tersely.

As the vans continued their journey, they eventually arrived at their destination—an abandoned mine nestled amidst a cluster of dilapidated log cabins.

The place was silent, seemingly abandoned. The only sound was the wind, but only if you weren't paying close enough attention.

Indeed, within moments, a group of armed Mexican men emerged from the wooden shacks, their eyes and automatic weapons trained on Todd. He cleared his throat and pretended nothing was amiss, knowing he would speak with their leader. It was his due, after all; he was becoming a big shot now.

Stepping out of his van, Todd greeted the men, led by their chief, known simply as "The Mexican". Todd motioned for Barney to join him, and together they approached the group. A strange tension filled the air as those beasts eyed each other, and they remained calm only because of their dirty common affairs.

"Howdy fellas! Y'all doin' alright?" Todd greeted them with a practiced smile.

The Mexican, puffing on a cigar, eyed Todd warily. "You're late," he grunted.

"Yeah, had me some trouble on the way over," Todd admitted. "But as y'all can see, I got ya two vans."

The Mexican nodded, and one of his men retrieved a briefcase from inside the cabin. Opening it, The Mexican revealed several bricks of cocaine. "We're fixin' to cross that border tonight," he announced. "We're bringin' una docena de chicos and some firepower."

"Ain't no thing," Todd assured him explaining, "Y'all go the usual route. My missus'll be there, and she'll make sure you pass. Barney! Get the money for these fine gentlemen."

Barney hurried to open Todd's van, fumbling through the numerous keys he carried with him. With the business settled, Todd prepared to ask The Mexican for a favor, but before he could speak, a commotion erupted from his van. A young girl, no more than thirteen, burst out, desperate to escape. She lunged at Barney, biting him on the neck.

"Fucking whore!" Barney cursed, kicking her to the ground. The man viciously attacked the girl, but the only thing that bothered

Todd was looking like fools in front of The Mexican. Todd intervened, halting Barney's assault.

"Hold it right there, fool! Ya had yer fun! I need her breathin'!"

"What is a white girl doing in my hideout?" The Mexican asked irritably.

As the tension mounted, Todd made a request of The Mexican: to keep the girl for him. Though reluctant at first, the cartel leader ultimately agreed, only because it would give his men something to do. He ordered his men to prepare for the journey, and Todd went to place a thick wad of bills in his hands. The Mexican took the money reluctantly, as if it were trash, and handed it to one of his subordinates. Amidst the chaos, the young girl lay on the ground, her whispered plea hanging in the air. "Dad…"

"You get the picture… Over all those years, Todd did nothing but indulge his criminal nature. Now, he found himself working with the cartel in drug trafficking. A real saint…"

In the vast expanse outside the town of Marfa, where the sky stretched endlessly, silence reigned supreme. Only the gentle rustle of leaves and the occasional chirp of a bird dared to break the tranquility. A small flyer fluttered lazily on the breeze, finally settling against a pair of women's shoes. Perched atop the hood of her car, Terry Brooke's attention was drawn to the flyer at her feet. With a quirk of curiosity on her lips, she leaned down to snatch it up. The flyer boasted the alluring promise: "Marfa: The Lowest Rents". It showcased a snapshot of a man named Todd, standing proudly beside some buildings.

Adjusting her sunglasses with a practiced flick, Terry lifted her gaze to the road sign ahead: "WELCOME TO MARFA! MAYOR: TODD BRANSON". A glimmer of intrigue danced in her green eyes as she slid into her car. With a smooth motion, she applied lipstick using the rearview mirror. Once satisfied with her makeup, Terry started her convertible and set off toward a new chapter of her life: Marfa.

A few minutes later, on the bustling main street, Terry strode with purpose, her head adorned with a stylish emerald scarf and her arm casually draped over a chic Marc Jacobs® bag. Her very presence commanded attention, turning heads as she gracefully navigated the sidewalk in her stiletto heels. Adjusting her sunglasses with an air of confidence, Terry's gaze fell upon a familiar sight: an office building emblazoned with the name: "Todd's Real Estate". Intrigued, she halted in front of the entrance, contemplating her next move, before confidently stepping inside.

As Todd focused on typing at his computer, his attention was abruptly diverted by the sight of Terry engaged in conversation with one of his staff members. With a curt nod to his employee, Todd rose from his desk and made his way over to them.

"I'll take it from here, Steve," Todd interjected, addressing the staff member who swiftly excused himself.

"Ms. Brooke, Todd Branson is the owner. He'll take good care of you," Steve informed Terry before stepping away.

"Thank you, kindly," she acknowledged with a polite smile.

"So, what can we do for you, Ma'am?" Todd inquired, extending his hand to Terry in a gesture of hospitality. She shook his hand firmly.

"My name is Terry Brooke. I need an apartment, preferably something cute and sunny."

"Well, you've certainly come to the right place," he assured her with a confident grin.

"I happen to be the mayor of this town, so whatever you need, consider it done." With a welcoming gesture, Todd invited Terry to follow him into his office.

"Thank you," Terry replied graciously as she entered his private domain. Once inside, Todd pulled out a chair for her and settled into one across from her. "Thanks!" she expressed her gratitude again, glancing around. The office reflected a somewhat eclectic personality. Hunting trophies hung incongruously alongside movie posters and antique weapons. An old rifle seemed to capture Terry's attention, momentarily diverting her focus from Todd, who cleared his throat.

"So... what brings you here?" Todd inquired, leaning back in his chair.

"A particularly bad divorce," Terry confessed with a sigh.

Todd offered a sympathetic smile.

"I'm sorry to hear that. Anyway... you have a budget in mind?"

"Not too much. I need to find a job," Terry replied honestly.

Todd's gaze momentarily wandered before he cleared his throat, refocusing on his client.

"My best friend Richard owns... well, an insurance company in town. I know they're short-staffed... Maybe..."

"Oh! Can I have his number? I've got experience in sales and building relationships with clients."

Todd nodded, acknowledging her enthusiasm, and adjusted the computer monitor to face her.

"Richard hates phones, but I'll introduce you to him in person." A greasy smile materialized on Todd's face. "But for now, let's get you sorted with your apartment."

And so it was, after a brief search, she found an expensive apartment. For reasons not fully explained, she could have it at a fifty percent discount, provided she was discreet, especially around the building superintendent. Naturally, Terry gladly accepted.

That same day, everything was done, or nearly so...

As Terry unloaded her car at her new apartment, she couldn't shake the feeling of being watched. Glancing over, she noticed the apartment superintendent, a seventy-five-year-old man with a sticky demeanor and a perpetually suspicious look. He was observing her with a strange expression. Though a bit unsettled, Terry pressed on toward her apartment, eager to settle in.

As the afternoon sunlight filtered through the half-open blinds, Terry's new apartment became a maze of unpacked boxes. Standing amidst the chaos, she carefully opened one cardboard box after another, eager to make her new space feel like home. Suddenly, a knock at the door interrupted her task. Terry turned to see Todd standing in the doorway, a friendly smile lighting up his face.

And that smile hinted at a sickly interest.

"Does the mayor always give a welcome to new folks like this?" Terry asked, a hint of amusement in her voice.

"Only the ones that catch my eye," Todd replied with a grin, his gaze briefly scanning the cluttered room.

Terry smiled back, a sense of warmth filling the room. She quickly smoothed down her hair, taking in Todd's presence. "It's perfect, thank you," she said sincerely, her eyes sweeping across the apartment. Todd nodded appreciatively, then shifted his weight slightly, his expression growing more serious.

"Anyway... ya still need work?" he inquired, his tone businesslike yet friendly.

BUSINESS

IN THE HEART of Marfa, Richard's insurance office saw little activity. Desks lined the space, illuminated by harsh, old fluorescent neon lights. Everything in that place was old and dedicated to frugality. Even the computers provided to the staff had yellowed with age, and the office appeared to be stuck in the eighties. Entering it felt like a step back in time. The few clients and the two employees usually lingered in a silence of pure, total boredom, but not that day.

That day one customer, visibly dissatisfied, flipped through a stack of documents while engaging in a heated discussion with one of the salesmen, and the tension was palpable.

Suddenly, the doors swung open, and Todd strode in, followed closely by Terry. The woman looked around curiously, appearing comfortable despite the mess that was the office. Richard, seated at his desk and engrossed in a game of computer solitaire, looked up as they entered. "Todd!"

"Hey, Rich! Let me introduce you to this lady here," Todd announced, gesturing towards Terry. Though dressed more suitably for moving than for an office, she maintained all her beauty and sensuality. The scent of her deodorant was a breath of fresh air in that place, which reeked of tobacco and rat poison. "She needs work. Says she's got a lot of experience." The other silent remark, insinuated by Todd, was appreciated by Richard, who smiled, his eyes lingering on the woman's chest for a long, long moment before the other man was forced to clear his throat. The insurance man's interest was piqued.

"A lot?"

"A lot," Todd confirmed with a nod.

Richard nodded understandingly before addressing the salesperson. "Martin, make way for this lady here." Martin, one of the two employees, was visibly surprised, but Richard insisted, "Let me check if she's ready for this."

With the boss's approval, Terry confidently assumed Martin's position, taking charge of the situation. She addressed the customer with professionalism and empathy, carefully examining the insurance contract. Her eyes scanned the documents and the client in front of her, and in no time, she slipped into her role as a salesperson. "Do you only want coverage while you're working, or do you want it to extend through retirement?" Terry asked, her voice confident yet compassionate.

The customer hesitated before responding, revealing personal concerns about providing for their family in the event of their passing. Terry listened attentively before offering a tailored solution.

Meanwhile, Richard and Todd watched everything like silent judges. However, Terry showed that she was at ease and that the job was truly in her wheelhouse. "Here's what you'll do for your loved ones..." With her persuasive charm, Terry guided the customer through the decision-making process, ultimately obtaining their signature on the contract.

As the transaction concluded, Richard's voice resonated from across the office with a few claps. "That was the most amazing sales pitch I've ever seen! Do you think you can train the other salespeople to do that?" The other employees exchanged glances as if to make sure they were still visible.

Terry smiled, a glimmer of satisfaction dancing in her eyes.

"I don't know what else to add; she was well-prepared..."

That same evening, after a loosely sketched, improvised first day of work, the whole group agreed to meet up at the local bar nestled on the edge of town. It exuded an air of familiarity, its weathered wooden exterior bearing the marks of countless years of patronage. Inside, the dim lighting cast a warm glow over the cozy interior, illuminating the worn barstools and tables scattered throughout the room. The low hum of conversation, mingled with the clinking of glasses and the occasional burst of laughter, created an ambiance of camaraderie and relaxation.

At a corner table, under the soft green glow of a lamp, Terry, Richard, and Todd sat together, engaged in lively conversation.

At that very moment, Barney arrived in his car. He parked in front of the bar and placed a "For Sale" sign on the windshield before entering.

"Howdy y'all!" Barney's voice boomed, drawing the attention of his friends.

"Howdy, Barney! How's it hangin'?" Todd greeted him warmly and this intrigued Barney, who noticed the new arrival next to Todd. "What's up? Did the mice in the garage put you in a bad mood again today?"

Everyone laughed, and when the laughter died down, Barney explained. "They went and stole one of my rides," he lamented.

"Which one of 'em?" Richard inquired.

"An old heap to fix up," Barney added with a sigh.

"So ain't no big deal... right?" Todd tried to reassure him.

"Yeah, jus' the trouble of talkin' to the law 'bout it," Barney grumbled.

Todd gestured for Barney to sit with them. "Well, let's see if we can take yer mind off it. This here's Terry!"

Terry got up from her seat and extended her hand to Barney. "Nice to make yer acquaintance!"

"The pleasure's all mine, darlin'," Barney replied with a nod as he settled into his seat.

Todd took a moment to boast about Barney's tenure as a car salesman. "Barney's been sellin' cars here for over 20 years, ever since we graduated high school."

"Y'all were high school buddies?" Terry inquired curiously.

"We were a crew. The best dang crew," Barney reminisced.

The conversation flowed freely, punctuated by the occasional clinking of glasses and bursts of laughter. It was a typical night among old and new friends. Yet, a certain erotic tension was already palpable in the air. Todd's gaze lingered longer and more intensely on Terry, and she didn't seem to mind.

TRAFFIC

UNDER THE COVER of night, City Hall stood tall and quiet, its impressive facade highlighted by the streetlights. A single police car, marked with the local emblem, came to a stop in front of the building.

Cindy, Todd's wife and the town's sheriff, stepped out of the vehicle. In her forties, she carried herself with an air of authority that demanded respect. Despite her heavy makeup, which accentuated her narrow features, there was no mistaking the strength and confidence in her posture.

The streets lay eerily quiet, with only a few solitary figures visible in the dim illumination. Breaking the stillness, a woman greeted Cindy warmly. "Hi, Cindy!"

"Howdy Julie! Is my husband around?".

"I reckon he's still holed up in his office,".

"Much obliged!" Cindy acknowledged before proceeding inside the city offices.

"Oh, yes, she was a police officer, but remember, the uniform doesn't define the person!"

In the warm ambiance of Todd's office, the soft glow of lamplight enveloped the room, creating an inviting atmosphere. The room was the epitome of American style. It was a replica of his work office, except that here he was forced to display the American flag—a symbol he did not recognize as legitimate. Anyway…

Seated at his desk, Todd was deeply engrossed in his work, hunched over his laptop, when Cindy entered, prompting a smile from him. "My Dear," He greeted her warmly.

After the initial exchange of pleasantries, Cindy quickly shut the door behind her. Her previously happy and serene expression shifted, revealing her true nature. Her face took on a dark and sinister look.

Cindy glanced around cautiously before leaning in closer to Todd, her voice lowered to a whisper. "You plannin' on headin' home early tonight?"

"Same old routine. How 'bout you?" Todd replied, trying to appear nonchalant despite the tension in the air. Laughter from nearby offices made them even more guarded in their conversation.

"I might have to pull a night shift to cover Thursday. They're short-handed," Cindy explained in a hushed tone.

Checking the door behind her again, she added,

"We've got an issue." The tension in Cindy's whisper conveyed the gravity of the situation. Shortly after, the two left the office and City Hall, heading towards her patrol car. The couple got in the car and, within a few blocks, reached their destination.

Arriving at the police station, the Bransons wasted no time as they hurried towards the entrance. As they reached the door, Todd felt a prickle of unease and scanned their surroundings, finding the street eerily empty. Cindy, sensing his hesitation, urged him, "Let's make it quick."

Once inside the station, the couple proceeded with the utmost expedience towards a particular room that must have been well guarded during the day. The room was where the police stored confiscated goods; here Cindy went straight to a locker and opened it. Todd found himself face-to-face with a brick of cocaine and recognized it immediately based on the blue sticker sealing it.

"Your stuff?" Cindy whispered, her voice barely audible.

Todd nodded solemnly as he retrieved the brick.

"That's right. It's mine," Todd admitted, his voice tinged with confusion.

As they exchanged worried glances, Cindy said, "It will take me a while, but I think I can recover it. The point is, that someone talked... They acted on a tip-off, Todd! That scares me."

Todd sighed angrily and said, "You make sure to recover it without anyone noticin', and don't dwell on it too much. The police stop drugs every day in this damn country!".

The mayor left shrouded in anger and disappointment.

"And indeed, it was true, especially in that area..."

The following day, in the twilight of a sweltering Marfa evening, the roar of an old Ford engine blended with the chirping of crickets. Todd soaked in the sun behind his sunglasses as he drove his customized muscle car. Despite the events of the previous night, he remained determined. After all, he was in charge here, and soon his influence would greatly increase.

In his mind, everything flowed smoothly; everything was perfect. All he had to do was end the day on a high note.

After a quick, rough parking job, Todd slipped out of the car with a weathered grace, a sprinkle of dust swirling around his worn boots.

A patrol officer noticed Todd's terrible parking, but with a quick exchange of glances, she decided to ignore the issue. After all, Todd was the mayor; he was the real authority around here. With his hat pulled down to shield his eyes from the scorching sun, he made his way toward Richard's insurance office.

Entering, Todd spotted Terry Brooke, now officially hired, absorbed in her computer display. With a friendly smile, he approached her workstation. "Howdy, Terry." His voice was rough but warm.

"I was thinkin' of talkin' insurance with you tonight... And maybe, afterward, we could take a ride along Route 90 and catch the Marfa Lights. Or we can swing by Donald Judd's exhibit while the sun sets."

Terry glanced up from her computer screen, her eyes twinkling with curiosity. "Sounds quite romantic," she replied, a hint of teasing in her tone.

"And it is," Todd agreed, his gaze intense. "And it would be even better... together."

A conspiratorial smile danced on Terry's lips as she leaned in slightly, her gaze burning with seduction. "And the wife?" she asked, a playful but loaded question.

Todd scratched the back of his neck nervously. "She's still at work—on the night shift at the station. But I don't plan on stayin' out too late."

Terry's smile dimmed slightly, and after a long couple of seconds, she said, "Perhaps next time," with a note of disappointment in her tone.

With a farewell nod, Todd stepped away from Terry's desk, saying, "Then next time it'll be! Mark my words!" He somehow seemed intimidating, not just confident, but Terry didn't seem to mind and smiled with satisfaction.

Todd walked away, heading back to his poorly parked car.

"Maybe he had trouble handling rejection... Well, he did have a lot of problems, and he caused plenty, too..."

That same night, Todd got into his car and headed to one of his usual meetings with The Mexican. He wasn't looking forward to it, having lost a drug deal that, although not significant, still stung a bit. He consoled himself with the thought that the money wasn't lost, just delayed. Lost in his thoughts, he found himself on a dark road that led him to the middle of nowhere. In a secluded clearing, the Mexicans were managing what appeared to be a small refugee camp.

The Mexican men, armed and imposing, surrounded a group of desperate immigrants, their faces etched with fear. The place reeked of exhaust from the numerous trucks and vans. The migrants' faces, filled with desperation and signs of violent treatment, didn't faze Todd as he boldly lit a cigarette and started towards the traffickers.

Suddenly, amidst the crowd of unfortunate people and sharp-eyed armed men, The Mexican appeared. Even though it was night, he wore a pair of sunglasses, and his movements seemed to be under the influence of some drug. That man was frightening, and unsettling to look at. Todd imagined he'd feel the same way facing a rabid dog.

The Mexican approached the mayor, surrounded by his men, as he yelled, "¡Pongan dos más en la camioneta! ¡Vi que hay espacio!"

A strong wind rose, sweeping up dust and even extinguishing Todd's cigarette. The Mexican barked orders, his voice cutting through the chaos as two unfortunate souls were forcibly seized and dragged away. Turning his steely gaze toward Todd, The Mexican demanded, "Mr. Mayor... Where's my cash?"

Unfazed by the intimidation tactic, Todd merely tilted his head and calmly re-lit his cigarette. "We had us a bit of a hiccup this go 'round. Nothin' that can't be fixed up in few days."

But The Mexican's patience wore thin as he repeated, more menacingly this time, "¿Dónde está mi dinero?"

"We'll get you yer cash soon enough," Todd assured him, his tone strained but resolute.

"But I need another shipment."

After a nod toward his bodyguard, The Mexican's demeanor shifted, his threats becoming more palpable.

A blade glinted in the moonlight.

The Mexican grabbed a machete from one of his men and pointed it at Todd's throat, threatening and shouting, "I think you're trying to fuck me over, cabrón!"

Todd, his nerves showing, attempted to defuse the tension. "Let's keep it real. Ain't no way in Hell yer gonna go shootin' the mayor of a town dead in the middle of the desert."

But The Mexican wasn't swayed, brandishing the machete and pressing it against Todd's throat with chilling resolve. "If you fuck with me, pendejo, I'll kill your friends, your family, and you last."

A tense standoff ensued, Todd's life hanging in the balance as blood trickled from the shallow wound on his neck. With his final warning, The Mexican withdrew, leaving Todd shaken but alive. Before departing, Todd dared to remind him, "Hey! I'm here for Bob too."

The Mexican halted upon hearing that name, sighing heavily before ordering one of his men to run off. He returned shortly after, accompanied by a crying child, who could not have been older than four years. The man handed the child to Todd, who took her as if she were a sack of potatoes—mere merchandise.

"Get me the money for the old load and this one, and do it pronto!"

With that, The Mexican vanished into the crowd, leaving Todd with the child under his arm. He sighed and then placed her in the trunk of his car before driving away.

"Yes, there were children involved, and believe me, that's what makes this story even more despicable!"

The same night, Todd and his friends sat in the local bar, eagerly awaiting their drinks. The soft strains of jazz music wafted from the jukebox, setting the mood for the evening.

A group of rebellious youths lingered, their laughter mingling with the music. They had been there for hours, having played hooky from school.

Seated at a corner table, Richard and Todd were immersed in tense conversation, their voices low.

Despite their complete lack of morals, they were true friends and did everything together. For this reason, Todd didn't hesitate to report the situation to his partner. In a way, they were codependent and knew well that one's collapse meant the end for the other. They needed to take action, though honestly, the situation wasn't out of control. Both had already made a lot of money and could cover the lost deal at any time.

Richard noticed Terry approaching their table with the beers and quickly steered the conversation away from their sensitive topic saying, "Alright, got it. Let me know if you need a hand."

Terry's arrival injected a burst of energy into the group. "These drinks are on me! Just a second, I'm going to touch up my makeup!" Terry declared cheerfully before stepping away. Todd's eyes followed Terry's graceful departure his interest evident as he turned to Richard.

Richard's attention was likewise drawn to her, his gaze lingering on her figure as he remarked, "She's got a real nice set of curves... I wonder what kinda' engine she's got under that skirt."

Todd chuckled, momentarily distracted.

"Speakin' of engines, you seen Barney around?"

Richard laughed heartily as he recounted Barney's recent frustrated attempts at installing security cameras. "That car they stole was just a hunk of junk... but Barney... is Barney, ya know...?"

The two had a good laugh at the thought of Barney, who, despite being so clumsy, was struggling with cables, drills, and ladders. It was a recipe for disaster. The conversation shifted to a more serious tone as Richard lowered his voice. "Can ya fill me in on the shipment that got seized?"

Todd responded thoughtfully, his tone reflective of the challenges ahead. "It's not a simple situation, but we'll figure something out eventually."

As the jukebox changed tunes, signaling the end of their conversation, Todd reassured his friend.

"I'll front the cash this time... but it looks like we'll have to wait before we can bring home the bacon." Their discussion concluded as Terry returned.

"Yeah, it was a night like any other... Or at least, it seemed that way."

A few minutes later as they exited the bar, Todd and Terry drifted noticeably closer.

"Alright, I gotta run. Todd, you and I'll see each other tomorrow!" Richard said. "And you, beautiful lady, I'll see you bright and early!" He kissed Terry's hand with suave charm. He hadn't been drinking much, so he couldn't blame the alcohol.

Todd felt a brief pang of jealousy, but within moments, he found himself alone with Terry. *"Such a shame—the moment's perfect, even magical. What's the word? Oh yeah, 'romantic'. Women like this sort of stuff,"* Todd thought. But then he was struck by a thought related to his duty, and that night he had to put off his primal urges. "I gotta go too."

Todd attempted to make a quick exit, but it seemed to disappoint Terry, who said, "What?! I was hopin' we could take a walk this time!"

"Unfortunately, I've got some work stuff to take care of! But I can assure you, next time we'll have our... 'walk','" Todd replied. His tone was heavy with alternate meaning and Terry bit her lip, perhaps thinking an inappropriate thought. They stood outside in silence for a long moment. "Okay, I'll see ya later!"

Todd's departure evoked a mix of emotions from Terry. He noticed that her smile seemed to mask a hint of sadness, causing him to smile to himself. He knew he was gaining power over her as he got into his car. The two stared at each other for a long moment. Eventually, Terry used the remote to unlock her own car. The flash of the lights briefly illuminated the dark street.

Todd made a silent promise of future encounters as Terry's car disappeared into the night, leaving him alone to ponder their intriguing connection.

In the depths of the night, Todd's car glided to a halt beside a solitary country house, its silhouette looming against the dim moonlit sky. Stepping out into the stillness, he surveyed his surroundings, his senses on high alert in the eerie quiet.

From the trunk of his car, Todd retrieved a shovel, its metal gleaming dully under the faint moon's glow. With determined steps, he advanced toward a lone tree, its twisted branches stretching like skeletal fingers toward the heavens. Beneath the tree's somber canopy, Todd plunged the shovel into the earth, each thrust accompanied by the unsettling sound of soil being displaced.

As the hole deepened, a shiver of unease crept over him, and he cast furtive glances around, half-expecting unseen eyes to be upon him. Finally, a metallic clang reverberated through the night as the shovel struck something solid.

Todd's pulse quickened with anticipation as he carefully unearthed a concealed container buried beneath the soil. With cautious hands, he lifted the lid, revealing a cache of money.

Swiftly, Todd pocketed a portion of the cash, leaving the rest undisturbed within its covert resting place.

With a mixture of trepidation and relief, he reburied the container, obscuring it once more beneath the Earth's surface. As he stood, surveying his handiwork, a sense of satisfaction washed over him. But his moment of triumph was fleeting, as a subtle prickling sensation at the back of his neck stirred a newfound wariness within him.

Gathering the shovel and the remaining money, Todd stowed them in the trunk of his car, his movements swift and purposeful. With a final glance over his shoulder, he slipped behind the wheel, igniting the engine and disappearing into the night's enigmatic embrace.

But a pair of watchful eyes lingered in the shadows, observing his every move with silent vigilance.

PARANOID

TERRY'S CAR CAME to a gentle stop in front of her apartment, its engine emitting a soft hum. With a quick check of her watch, she emerged onto the pavement, the click of her heels punctuating the stillness of the night.

Approaching the superintendent's apartment, Terry rapped lightly on the door, the sound reverberating softly in the quietude of the night. The door creaked open, revealing the fatigued form of the superintendent, his demeanor worn yet obliging.

"I'm Terry, from Apartment 9D," she explained, her voice tinged with a note of apology. "Seems I've misplaced my keys."

The superintendent responded quickly, clearly familiar with Terry. He reached for a heavy keychain, his movements showing both resignation and duty. "Here we go," he said, his voice steady. "I'll get the door for you." As he fumbled with the keys, Terry watched, her expression a mix of impatience and curiosity. "Let's get this done," he muttered, leading Terry towards her apartment with a sense of reluctant obligation.

In the hallway, the superintendent adeptly unlocked the door, allowing her to step inside with a brief nod of acknowledgment. Terry, appreciative of the assistance, offered a quick explanation for her forgetfulness. "I left my key in my other purse," she remarked with a wry smile, her chagrin evident.

With a word of gratitude, Terry bid the superintendent good-night, watching as he retreated down the hallway. As the door clicked shut behind him, she released a sigh of relief, the tension of the moment dissolving as she kicked off her shoes and sank into the welcoming embrace of her apartment.

After a few seconds, she began to strip off her formal clothes.

"Revenge."

As the sun began to illuminate the cityscape, a grim tableau unfolded within the confines of Richard's insurance office. Richard's lifeless body hung from a noose, casting a macabre pending shadow on the floor.

Detective Kevin Sun, a burly middle-aged Caucasian man, accompanied by his partner James Reyes, a wiry Mexican immigrant in his mid-thirties, entered the office with somber expressions. Sherrif Branson stood nearby, her eyes brimming with sorrow at the loss of her dear friend.

Surveying the scene with a keen eye, Detective Sun noted the absence of security cameras—a detail that would undoubtedly complicate their investigation. As he examined the bruising around Richard's neck and the signs of a head injury, his partner observed the lack of forced entry, hinting at a deeper mystery surrounding the insurance man's death.

The two detectives communicated without words to each other, and it was Cindy who first broke the silence. Her voice carried a false sorrow. "I must inform my husband... Sorry, Richard was his best friend, and for me, it's horrible." Her voice trembled with grief as she tearfully excused herself from the room. The detectives exchanged a knowing glance, understanding the weight of her burden.

With Cindy gone to deliver the tragic news to Todd, Sun and Reyes turned their attention to the shocked employees gathered outside the office. The two detectives emerged and began to observe the faces of the employees who were waiting to know what to do. "My name is Detective Sun, and this is my partner, Detective Reyes. I assume you're all familiar with the procedure from movies, so let's get started immediately." Kevin addressed them with a tone of authority, his badge prominently displayed. "Who among you was the last to see Richard alive?"

Terry, visibly shaken, stepped forward, her voice quivering as she recounted her last encounter with Richard. "Okay, let's start with you, but no one leaves town, and make yourselves available for further questioning, understood?" Everyone nodded in agreement.

Soon after, Terry found herself in the muted ambiance of a quaint coffee shop, facing Detective Sun.

The weight of their conversation hung heavy in the air, akin to the aroma of freshly brewed coffee. "So... you had a drink?" Detective Sun's voice was measured, probing for details.

Terry nodded solemnly, her mind returning to the night before with Richard and Todd. "Yes, it was myself and Todd, Richard's friend," she confirmed.

Detective Sun furrowed his brow slightly. "Todd. Todd the mayor?"

"Yes, the mayor," Terry replied, a note of apprehension creeping into her voice.

Leaning forward, Detective Sun pressed on.

"And then what?" he inquired, ready to document her account.

Taking a deep breath, Terry began to recount the events of the night, her words deliberate and measured.

"Well, I had to head home," she started, her voice trailing off momentarily as she recalled the mundane details of her evening.

"Can anyone vouch for your whereabouts?" Detective Sun interjected, his gaze steady as he awaited her response.

Terry paused, her mind racing as she searched for a corroborating alibi. "Yes, the building superintendent; he had to let me in since, I forgot my keys."

The detective made a note in his diary, his expression inscrutable.

"And what time was that?" he probed further, his tone neutral.

"I'm not entirely sure, but it was right after we finished our drinks, so around eight-fifteen p.m.," Terry answered, with a hint of uncertainty in her voice. "By the way, is it being treated as a suicide?" she added, her curiosity getting the better of her.

The detective took a long moment to scrutinize her face, putting his notepad in the pocket of his trench coat. "Forensics will provide more insight," Sun replied cryptically, his gaze thoughtful as he pondered the implications of Terry's statement.

In Todd's house, a tense atmosphere enveloped the room as Cindy broached the subject of the detectives' impending visit.

"The Detectives're gonna have a word with you. Try to think of anythin' that might give 'em a hand," Cindy urged with concern.

Todd, reclining on the couch with a cigarette in hand, listened intently, but with a hint of irritation. "Ah, yeah, I'm on the list as one of the folks that saw him last," he acknowledged with a simple shrug. Maybe it would have been strange for anyone else, yet Todd was who he was. He had lost his best friend and seemed to be merely annoyed by the whole matter.

Before they could dwell further, a sudden knock at the door disrupted their conversation. The sound reverberated through the silent room, amplifying the tension that hung heavy in the air. Todd glanced at Cindy, a silent exchange passing between them, before he rose from the couch and made his way to the door.

Just before opening the door, Todd checked his facial expression in a mirror and transformed his complete disinterest into a devastated and convincingly believable look. With a sense of apprehension gnawing at his gut, he reached for the doorknob. The door swung open, revealing the figures of Detectives Sun and Reyes. Todd's heart skipped a beat, his mind racing with unspoken fears and uncertainties.

"We're the detectives investigatin' Richard's death. I believe your wife had a chance to inform you. I'm Kevin Sun, and this is..."

Cindy immediately assumed the role of the gracious hostess. "Oh, come in! Wasn't expectin' you this soon," she exclaimed, stepping aside for Todd to allow them entry. The sherriff was keen on giving the impression that they were a picture-perfect couple, with no troubles in the world. In truth, they were damn well made for each other.

"Come in, come in. Have a seat!" Todd greeted them warmly, though a hint of unease flickered in his eyes as they settled onto the couches.

"Can I offer y'all somethin' to drink?" Cindy kept playing the part of the perfect housewife, but Kevin declined, saying, "No thanks. We won't be here long, and we don't want to be a bother."

The weight of impending questions hung heavy in the air. "So, Mayor, we just wanted to briefly go over what happened last night... can you recall anything out of the ordinary?" Detective Sun inquired, his pen poised over his notepad.

"No, I mean, it was a normal night," Todd replied, his tone casual but with a hint of tension.

"We went for some beers and then went home. Richard was fine."

There was a brief pause, and in the silence, the detective started to scribble notes. "So you drank some beers and went straight home," he summarized.

"We got home around the same time: nine o'clock."

"I can attest to that," Cindy interjected, her voice steady.

The detective glanced at his notes, then back at Todd. "So, you left the bar, when?" he pressed, his gaze penetrating.

Todd hesitated, his eyes darting around the room. "I can't exactly remember," he admitted reluctantly.

"Well, we have Richard disarming his security at eight-sixteen in the office," the detective revealed, watching Todd closely.

"Oh yeah, he went straight to the office. I took a walk," Todd explained, a touch of defensiveness in his tone.

"So, you didn't go straight home after you left the bar—you took a walk," Sun noted, jotting something down.

"Well, I mean, I went straight home once I got in my car. I had a few beers, and I don't like driving drunk," Todd clarified, his explanation somewhat strained.

"How long was that walk?"

"I don't remember, thirty... forty minutes maybe..." Todd replied, his voice trailing off.

"Long walk," Reyes chimed in, a hint of skepticism in his tone.

"Was Richard drunk as well?"

"No, Richard knew he had to work, so he didn't drink much," Todd answered, his gaze shifting uncomfortably.

"Did Terry drink much?" the detective asked, causing Cindy to glance over with curiosity.

"Who's Terry?" The sheriff interjected, her brow furrowing in confusion.

"Richard's new head of sales. She's a stand-up gal," Todd replied quickly, though his discomfort was evident. "I'm guessin' she didn't have much—she probably didn't want to get plastered in front of her boss—but I wasn't keepin' tabs on how much she drank." Todd ended his sentence with a final smile, but neither of the detectives returned it, which made the hairs on the back of his neck stand up.

Kevin resumed speaking. "Well, Terry mentioned that she got home around eight p.m., so that means you all left together?" the detective probed further, his eyes fixed on Todd.

"Yes, we all left 'round the same time," the mayor confirmed, his response tinged with uncertainty.

"Do you know where she lives?" Sun inquired, his gaze unwavering.

"Yes! Well, I mean... I'm Mr. Real Estate in this town, and the mayor," Todd replied, a touch of defensiveness creeping into his voice. The detective nodded, making a note in his pad.

The tension in the room was palpable, but despite it, a few minutes later, the encounter came to an end. The detectives exchanged pleasantries with the couple before making their way back to their car.

Todd watched them leave through the blinds. He knew he hadn't made a good impression, that he had fumbled for a moment, but he also knew he was innocent, so he had little to fear.

Once seated inside the car, a heavy silence descended with the weight of the detectives' suspicions.

"Lyin' through his teeth," Sun muttered, evidently frustrated. "But maybe he's involved with the woman and didn't want to get busted in front of his wife."

Reyes nodded in agreement, his expression thoughtful.

"And Terry's got a witness..."

Sun leaned back in his seat, contemplating their next move. "You're right. There's gotta be somethin' else."

"So, it's the usual routine, huh?" Reyes remarked with a resigned sigh. "Let's go question some friends and family, shall we?"

"Let's go," Sun replied tersely, his jaw set with determination as he shifted the car into gear, pulling out onto the street.

"And so, Todd found himself smack dab in the middle of a murder investigation he sure as heck hadn't seen coming."

As the detectives approached Barney's house, the morning sun cast a warm glow over the quiet neighborhood. They noticed the flicker of lamplight through the curtains, indicating activity inside despite the early hour. The muffled sounds of a heated argument drifted out, prompting uneasy glances between Sun and Reyes.

"I'll kill ya, God as my witness! You're just a damn, retarded whore!" The sound of breaking dishes followed the threats.

"Come on, ring the dang doorbell! Maybe they'll calm down a bit..." Reyes muttered, gesturing towards the door.

Detective Sun nodded in agreement and pressed the doorbell, the chime echoing through the serene morning air. Instantly, the commotion inside ceased, replaced by an eerie stillness. After a tense moment, the door creaked open, revealing Barney, who eyed them cautiously. The man was practically in his underwear. Behind him was his wife, a gaunt woman with a helpless look and tear-filled eyes.

"Who're you?" Barney's voice was strained, his brow furrowed in confusion.

Detective Sun raised his badge and introduced himself and his partner. "My name is Kevin Sun. This is my partner, Detective James Reyes. We're here to ask you a few questions regarding your friend Richard."

Barney's expression darkened at the mention of Richard's name. "Richard? What happened?"

With a serious voice, Detective Sun delivered the news. "I'm sorry to inform you that your friend has passed away. We just wanted to ask you a few questions and see if you could tell us where you were last night."

Barney hesitated for a moment, his eyes clouded with grief and disbelief.

"I 'bin workin' all day in ma shop, installin' alarms and cameras. Got the footage too, if y'all wan' it."

The detectives exchanged a knowing glance, acknowledging Barney's cooperation before proceeding with their questioning.

GETTING WORSE

THE ATMOSPHERE AT Todd's house was charged with tension, the aftermath of their encounter with the detectives igniting a storm of discussions. Cindy, now alone with her husband, seethed with a jealousy that bordered on madness. Todd attempted to address the situation, but his words seemed to evaporate in the heated atmosphere. "Well, I guess we should just be more careful".

Cindy stood up to face Todd and remained silent for a few moments. Then, like a bolt of lightning, her voice sliced through the air, sharp and furious. "WHO THE FUCK IS TERRY?" Her anger was palpable, her frustration boiling over.

"She's just an employee at Richard's office. You don't know her 'cause she ain't been here long." Todd's response was stoic, his demeanor unwavering despite the sharp slap that met his cheek. "Cut it out, woman!" he snapped, seizing her hands to block another strike.

But Cindy was relentless, her struggles against his hold fueled by her jealousy and rage. As Todd explained his actions from the previous night, mixing lies and truth, Cindy's anger began to dissipate, replaced by a grim understanding of the gravity of the situation. After all, Todd had gone to get the money from the secret stash; it was only natural that he wanted to stay vague about his whereabouts. Cindy seemed to calm down. The tale he weaved was working.

Sighing to calm herself, the woman said, "Pay The Mexican as soon as possible... I wouldn't want Richard to be some kind of cautionary tale," she urged, her voice tinged with concern. Silence hung heavy between them as they both struggled to regain their composure.

Todd, feeling overwhelmed by Cindy's presence, stepped out, slamming the door shut behind him. There, alone in the driveway with his frustration, he discovered that the trunk of his car had been tampered with. His belongings were scattered in disarray, and the cash was gone. In a fit of rage, he pounded his fist against the empty trunk, his curses echoing into the air. "Shit! Shit! Shit!" he shouted, his frustration boiling over as he kicked the vehicle.

Cindy heard the noises and looked out the kitchen window to see her husband apparently going crazy. She caught his eye and the two stared at each other for a long moment. Fortunately, there was no one else on the street.

Todd tried to compose himself, knowing he absolutely couldn't afford to attract attention.

"At that point, it was impossible to pretend that everything was still okay."

In the chilly storage room, the coroner swung open the heavy door, revealing Richard's lifeless body laid out on a stainless-steel table. As the cold air spilled into the room, the detectives stepped forward, their breath forming misty clouds in the frigid atmosphere.

"The victim," the coroner began, gesturing toward Richard's body, "showed signs of blunt force trauma to the back of his skull, and the ligature marks suggest that he was hanged. Although the blow to his skull may have knocked him unconscious, it wasn't fatal." With a gloved hand, the coroner pointed out the bruise on Richard's head, evidence of the violence inflicted upon him.

"Do you have anything else?" Sun asked, his voice a low murmur in the solemn room.

"I can tell you that he suffered a slow death," the coroner replied, his tone serious.

"Perhaps it was an oversight by the killer... or a deliberate over-kill," Reyes interjected, his brow furrowed with concern.

"Have you determined what they used to knock him out?"

The coroner shook his head. "No, but it had to be a small, heavy object with no sharp edges—maybe a paperweight."

With a heavy silence settling over them, the detectives took one last glance at Richard's lifeless body, the weight of their investigation bearing down on them like a shroud.

In the same hours, amid the desolate countryside, Todd's car pulled up to the abandoned house where he had hidden the money. His gaze fixed on the solitary shovel standing under the shade of the gnarled tree. With a sense of unease gnawing at him, Todd exited the car and strode toward the tree. As he approached, his heart sank at the sight of a freshly dug hole. Realization dawned upon him like a chilling breeze—the money was gone. With a sense of urgency, Todd retrieved his phone and punched in Cindy's number. Not even a single ring.

"Hi, this is Cindy! Leave a message, and I'll call you back!"

Beep.

"Cindy, we got a fucking problem!" Todd's voice crackled through the line, urgency coloring every word. After leaving the message, Todd remained frozen in place. Dozens of thoughts and worries were now making their way into his heart and carving a hole of fear in his stomach.

"How does it feel, Todd? Oh, I wish you could hear my hearty laughter."

The following morning, at the local watering hole, the bartender, Ryan, prepared for another day of business. The wooden bar, with its polished oak counter and shelves lined with bottles, was a staple of the community. That bar was the last place where Richard was seen alive. Ryan was arranging the tables outside when he noticed the two detectives stepping out of their car.

"Good morning. Here to ask a few questions—won't take long," Kevin said, his tone casual yet authoritative.

"Y'all want any coffee?" Ryan offered hospitably.

"No thanks," Kevin declined, his focus undivided.

"We just have some questions about some of your patrons," James added, his gaze probing.

"This about Richard's death?" Ryan guessed, his interest piqued as he led them inside.

"He was here—him, the mayor, and... Terry. Right?" James asked, seeking confirmation.

"Yeah... the new girl at the insurance office," The bartender confirmed, his memory sharp.

"Was there anything out of the ordinary you noticed?" Reyes inquired, his curiosity piqued.

"Nope. Same ol' same ol'..." Ryan's demeanor was casual yet guarded as he wiped down the counter.

"How long did they stay?" Kevin probed further, his gaze unwavering.

"Maybe forty-five minutes? Enough time for a few beers, and a cocktail for the lady altogether," Ryan recalled.

"Did the mayor show any signs of aggression? Was Richard visibly upset?" Reyes pressed, seeking clarity.

"Look, they usually play rough, but nothin' outta the ordinary, really."

The detectives exchanged a knowing glance, silently urging the bartender to continue.

"Do you recall what they were squabblin' about?" Kevin prompted.

"Not exactly. I think they were talkin' about money at some point, but I wasn't payin' much attention," Ryan admitted, his expression thoughtful.

"Who paid?" Kevin queried.

"Lady did," Ryan replied, his gaze drifting to a box beneath the bar.

"You got the receipt?" Kevin asked, keenly interested.

"Sure do." The bartender retrieved the box and sifted through its contents with practiced ease. Finally, he procured the desired receipt and handed it over to Kevin, his movements deliberate and precise. Detective Sun examined the receipt for confirmation, but his mind had already wandered into a myriad of possible next steps in his investigation.

A few minutes later, the detectives stepped out into the blinding daylight. Kevin cast his contemplative gaze up and down the bustling street, his thoughts veiled behind a mask of introspection. Life in Marfa flowed as usual on this sleepy morning.

"Which way ya think Todd took his walk?" James inquired, breaking the silence.

"I don't know, but he's lucky if he just needs one beer to get drunk," Kevin mused, his tone tinged with humerous skepticism.

"Where we headed?" Reyes prompted.

"Let's go get a warrant to check his accounts," Kevin decided resolutely. The two detectives made their way back to their car.

That same morning, at the police station, the detectives poured over documents with meticulous intensity. During their search through thousands of pages, Sherrif Branson happened to pass by. Careful not to be noticed, she seized the opportunity to see what the detectives were focusing on. Taking advantage of their brief coffee break, she slipped quietly into the room. She found herself holding her husband's financial documents. Todd seemed to be under particular scrutiny by the two detectives. After a lingering moment, Cindy turned away, her steps measured and hesitant as she retreated from the room.

With a glance back at the detectives near the coffee vending machine, she disappeared into the labyrinthine of corridors. The sheriff wanted to warn her husband, but at that very moment, he was in the company of Terry in a less-frequented diner of Marfa.

Terry carried two cups of coffee to their booth, her empathetic gaze fixed on Todd's troubled face. There was a certain sadness in the air, at least from Terry's perspective, while Todd seemed lost in his thoughts.

"I'm real sorry 'bout Richard. I could tell y'all were close," Terry offered with genuine sympathy.

With a heavy sigh, Todd acknowledged the sentiment, his frustration evident in the creased lines of his brow. As Terry reached out to touch his hand, his phone rang out, loud and insistent. It was Cindy—strange that she was calling this time of day. With a swift motion, Todd answered the call to hear, "The detectives have a warrant to investigate yer accounts. Best watch yerself!"

Cindy's warning echoed through the phone before the call abruptly disconnected. Todd's expression tightened, a mixture of concern and resolve clouding his features as he absorbed the weight of his wife's words. Terry hadn't heard, but Todd worried that his expression might betray what was brewing inside. "Sorry, it's an emergency. I gotta go."

"Alright. See you at the funeral?" Terry's question caught Todd off guard. It took him a moment to gather his thoughts and say before leaving, "Oh yeah, the funeral... See ya there!"

"Y'all see? Todd wasn't even thinking about Richard; he was the least of his worries. But then again, can you blame him?"

Under the somber gray sky of the cemetery, mourners gathered around as the coffin was reverently lowered into the waiting earth, marking their final farewell to Richard. Todd stood among them, his expression a mixture of disbelief and sorrow. He shared a silent exchange with Barney, who mirrored his feelings. In her uniform, Sherriff Branson observed the scene with a solemn gaze. Her attention occasionally drifted towards Terry, who stood nearby engaged in conversation with a colleague. As the priest's voice rose in prayer, the newcomer, draped in elegant black attire, dipped her chin and folded her hands respectfully.

"Eternal rest grant unto him, oh Lord, and let perpetual light shine upon him..." The priest's words hung heavy in the air as clumps of dirt were ceremoniously cast upon the coffin by the mourners. Todd dutifully participated in the ritual, but his actions betrayed a sense of detachment, his huffing breath revealing a restless boredom amidst the solemnity of the occasion. And so, the funeral came to an end, with the detectives observing everything from a distance.

An hour later, still dressed in funeral attire, Todd stood alone in the middle of a deserted country road, seemingly waiting for someone. His car was parked behind him while his gaze was drawn to the vast expanse of the desert stretching out before him, the smoke from his cigarette curling lazily in the air. Soon, Barney's sleek sports car became visible in the distance, kicking up a cloud of dust. In less than a minute, Barney pulled up, and he approached Todd with a concerned expression. "How you holdin' up?" he inquired, his tone sympathetic.

Todd's eyes betrayed the weight of his thoughts as he responded, "I was thinkin' about Richard. I'd like to know who killed him."

Barney nodded in understanding. "Got any suspicions?" he asked.

"A lot," Todd admitted, a hint of frustration in his voice. "But sadly, my conscience ain't clear."

"Why'd you wanna see me?" Barney inquired.

Todd flicked his cigarette to the ground before responding, his voice low and urgent. "I got a problem and need yer help…"

"Alright, spill," Barney encouraged.

Todd hesitated briefly before divulging, "The detectives think I killed Richard. They're breathin' down my neck. I need you to go to The Mexican to settle a small debt."

Barney was absorbing the information, but he was confused somehow. He was a person you could use with just a little effort, and Todd knew it well. He knew there was a risk to take, and he wouldn't take it of course, so Barney was perfect. "Just tell me how much you need," the car salesman said, as the mayor was already lost in thought.

"I need a hundred grand," Todd admitted, conscious of the weight of his request.

"How soon do you need it?" asked his friend, obviously concerned.

"As soon as possible," Todd responded urgently. "Anymore stallin' and I'm probably gonna end up in a ditch somewhere."

Barney nodded in understanding, already moving towards his car. "Alright, but I gotta hit up the bank—I ain't got that much cash."

"Safety deposit box?" Todd asked, to make sure not to leave any traces.

"Sure. Just gotta swing by home real quick to grab the key," Barney confirmed as he settled into the driver's seat.

As Barney drove away, Todd watched him go, a sense of urgency clouding his expression. After a moment's hesitation, the mayor headed towards his own car, his mind consumed by the weight of his troubles. But at least this one was done. A significant problem was finally solved.

OR MAYBE NOT...

IN STARK CONTRAST to the serene desert landscape, forensics teams converged on a remote area outside of town, where the wreckage of a red sports car lay twisted and broken against the unforgiving terrain.

The forensic team and the police were already on the scene.

The detectives and Sherriff Branson stood grimly beside the wreckage, their eyes fixed on Barney's lifeless form within the mangled vehicle. As Cindy shared the gory details of the discovery, Kevin nodded in silent acknowledgment.

"Some bikers caught sight of the smoke and called it in."

A few vultures circled patiently overhead, adding to the ominous atmosphere. The detectives observed the scene with a critical eye, noting the telltale signs of foul play amidst the wreckage.

One of the officers drew Cindy's attention, allowing James to speak freely to his partner, albeit in a low voice, his words heavy with conviction. "I ain't fond of havin' a suspect's wife hangin' around... Anyway... I'll be damned if that's an accident. Someone ran him off the road. There's a killer on the loose," Reyes declared, his tone resolute. Kevin nodded in agreement, his gaze drawn to the broken guardrail and the desolate road beyond. A couple of minutes later,

James noticed a trail of liquid on the road. "Brake fluid," he muttered to himself, but the other detective remained perplexed.

Suddenly, Kevin's voice cut through the stillness of the desert.

"Hey, Sheriff! Any idea where that road leads?"

Cindy's response was tinged with uncertainty as she admitted, "Nowhere. I mean, it's for kids and those who like to go sit in the middle of nowhere."

But Kevin's instincts told him otherwise, his gaze lingering on the road ahead as he whispered, "Oh, all roads lead somewhere..."

Reyes captured the moment with a photo, the evidence of their investigation unfolding amidst the stark beauty of the desert landscape.

That same afternoon, the detectives paid a visit to Barney's wife. They found themselves in the living room of a house that was, in some way, "touched by madness". They were warmly welcomed by the woman, who didn't seem at all distraught. For a long moment, they waited for the tea that she had insisted on preparing.

As they began sipping the tea, the two detectives confronted the widow, who appeared surprisingly calm given the circumstances. Sunlight filtered through the lace curtains, casting a warm glow over the room. The faint aroma of freshly brewed tea lingered in the air as she delicately took a sip from a china cup. "Ma'am, we'll try not to take up too much of your time. Just please tell us if anyone comes to mind who harbored any animosity or resentment towards your husband," Kevin said.

The woman almost smiled, as if the question were all too obvious, but she held back, wiping that smile from her face, opting instead for some kind of performance. "I know, I mean... I know Barney sold some rides he maybe shouldn't have sold, and folks got mad. Heard they jacked one too... but..." she began, her voice trailing off as she searched her memory.

"Jacked? When?" Reyes leaned forward with interest, his eyes focused on her.

"I don't remember," the widow admitted with a slight furrow of her brow, her memory failing her momentarily.

Detective Sun, ever diligent, jotted down notes in his leather-bound diary, the scratch of his pen the only sound in the room for a moment.

"Do you know what type of vehicle?" James inquired, his curiosity driving the conversation forward.

"No."

"The color?" He prompted, his tone gentle yet probing.

"It was black… and old," Barney's wife responded calmly, her eyes distant as she tried to recall the details. There was a hint of amusement in her voice. The two detectives exchanged glances, sensing something unusual in the woman's demeanor. It was as though she was struggling to suppress a laugh, her composure slipping for a moment.

"Any threats?" Reyes redirected the conversation, his focus unwavering.

"Oh, sure, but nothin' 'real'—just angry messages. I don't think nothin' serious," she reassured them, her tone casual yet tinged with fake concern.

The detective leaned forward, his posture attentive. "Ma'am, we got his phone. It was on his body. If you would be so kind as to make us privy to the password, maybe we can look through his device. I mean... without havin' to wait."

"I ain't got his password. I ain't got no talent for technology. Neither did Barney... I always figured he might have a side thing..." the widow admitted, a fleeting smile crossing her lips before she quickly returned to feigning sadness, her eyes betraying a hint of mischief.

Kevin's interest was piqued by her statement. "What gave you those suspicions?" he probed further, his gaze sharp as he searched for clues.

"He would always disappear," Barney's wife replied cryptically, her smile returning momentarily before fading once more into a mask of sorrow.

The detective was deeply struck by those words, but many years of practice kept him from rushing to conclusions. In any case, he knew that there was something rotten in the town—something that had been covered up with profound dedication.

That same morning, the two detectives pressed on with their investigation, swiftly retracing Barney's recent movements, thanks to witness accounts and footage from security cameras—footage which they diligently studied to glean any clues. A monitor displayed grainy black-and-white bank security footage, capturing the movements of a man entering the main doors. It was Barney.

"This is the last footage of Barney alive," James' voice echoed through the room. The images on the screen raced forward, showing Barney exiting the bank with a bag in hand.

"He took somethin' from his safety deposit box, right?" Sun mused aloud.

"Looks like it," Reyes confirmed, adding, "That bag went missin', and, once again, we ain't got nothin'."

"We still have the fact that the bag is missin', which probably means it was hidin' somethin'."

A deep silence fell, and Kevin concluded that the best course of action in such cases was to resort to "old-fashioned methods". "I reckon we should take a gander at everyone's background, just to get an idea of who we're workin' with," he suggested.

James nodded in agreement, zooming in on the images, trying to discern any details about the bag's contents. "I reckon there's money stashed away in there for sure…"

After finishing their analysis of the footage, the detectives requested access to the archives. They were assisted by a cowboy-looking officer named Bob, who was both elderly and remarkably kind-hearted.

"This here's the archives, fellas," Bob announced, after introducing himself with a warm smile. He ushered them into a small, dimly lit room filled with rows of dusty files.

"Luckily for y'all, there's not much to sift through. But if ya need a hand, don't hesitate to give me a holler," he offered before leaving them to their investigation. As the neon lights flickered on, illuminating the archive room, the detectives began their meticulous review of the files.

An hour later, they shed their jackets in the stuffy room, Kevin lighting a cigarette as they poured over the documents. The hour had turned into two, then three, and the stress began to loosen their shirt collars. James had become a bit less tolerant than usual. "Hey now, smokin' ain' allowed here," he reminded his partner.

"Yeah, good things always seem to be short-lived," the detective remarked, leaving the cigarette on the ashtray before adding, "Did ya come across anythin' interestin'?"

James peered through prescription glasses at an old case file.

"For the most part, small crimes. The city is small, but… I've got an old rape file here: 'Daly Flores'", he reported, flipping through the pages.

"They interviewed Todd and… some of his peers," he continued, catching the other detective's attention.

"Rape, huh?" Kevin murmured thoughtfully.

"It's a cold case. Ain't nobody found guilty," James replied, a note of skepticism in his voice.

"So... to recap: Todd's financials are good, at least as far as he tells the IRS," Kevin summarized.

"We ain't got nothin' but our suspicions about him," James admitted with a sigh.

"Might be high time to pull some strings," Kevin suggested, sharing a meaningful look with his partner as they contemplated their next move.

"So… what're we gonna do?" James asked.

The older detective answered with a mischievous smile.

The sound of a heavy clock was all that could be heard inside the Branson residence. The couple ate dinner without exchanging many glances. It was some kind of soup, which Todd didn't seem to enjoy much. The air was heavy with worries that refused to turn into a conversation, but still...

"Detectives're goin' over everything," Cindy remarked, breaking the quiet.

"Hmm," Todd grunted in response, his expression grim.

"I checked out the files on their desk..." Cindy trailed off, her voice low.

"And? What they got?" He leaned forward, his eyes narrowing.

"They definitely pinned you as a suspect."

"I ain't guilty, and they ain't got no proof," Todd declared firmly.

"Yeah, but ya can't have them detectives snoopin' around," she cautioned.

Todd's temper flared, his frustration boiling over.

"You make it sound easy, but trust me, messin' with the Mexicans ain't no walk in the park. He's expectin' his cash, and them ain't the kind of folks ya wanna cross," he warned, his voice rising.

"You think The Mexican offed Richard and Barney?"

"I dunno," Todd admitted, his voice tinged with uncertainty.

"You don't know?!" Cindy's voice rose in disbelief.

"Barney had the cash to take to 'em," Todd defended.

"Ain't nothin' in the ride..." Cindy countered.

"I was countin' on it," Todd conceded, his frustration evident.

"What're ya gonna do? Even if it weren' The Mexican, somebody's droppin' y'all like flies and you're next, Todd! Ya gettin' this, Todd?" Cindy pressed, her voice urgent.

Todd's frustration reached a breaking point, and he slammed his fist onto the table, causing his wife to jump with fright. "Well, no shit, Sherlock! Yer no help to me if you just keep pointin' out the obvious!" the mayor snapped.

The sheriff rose from her seat, her expression tense with determination.

"Don't let 'em find out about that Mexican. Git yerself some cash and make it happen!" she ordered before storming out of the room.

Todd snorted, watching through the window as she stomped to her car.

Meanwhile, James observed the house from a distance, crouching next to Todd's car. With stealth, he discreetly placed a GPS tracker under the wheel housing before slipping away around the corner to where Kevin waited.

"Placed. Receiving?"

"Yeah, it's comin' through!" Kevin confirmed.

GUILTY!

SEEING HIMSELF BACKED into a corner, Todd had no choice but to sell one of his many properties—an old cottage he had never used but could now turn into quick cash. It stung a bit, feeling like a failure—a sort of demotion in his criminal career. Nevertheless, he was selling, and he had to deal with the lawyer who had long shown interest in the property.

He was a rich-born jerk, in Todd's eyes, who only had to speak to be loathsome. And unfortunately, at that moment, he was speaking. "I gotta say, I was real surprised when ya told me ya wanted to sell it."

The cottage, nestled in the woods, appeared quaint and peaceful under the midday sun. Its weathered exterior hinted at years of stories whispered among the trees.

Todd, dressed somberly in funeral attire, stood outside the cottage alongside Ozzy, the lawyer and buyer. He was a portly man with a booming voice and a penchant for flashy jewelry that clashed with his tacky Hawaiian shirt. His laughter echoed through the woods, incongruous with the serene backdrop.

Todd responded, each word uttered reluctantly. "I ain't never had a chance to use it. Land all around the river's included. Ya gotta fix up the fence in some spots, but the price I'm givin' ya is a steal!" Todd explained earnestly, his words a stark contrast to Ozzy's brash demeanor. Yet, despite his rough exterior, there was a shrewdness in his eyes that hinted at his success in the cutthroat world of business.

"My youngins are gonna go nuts!" Ozzy exclaimed, a satisfied grin on his face as he surveyed the cottage. He ran his hand through his greasy hair, leaving behind a trail of a strange floral scent.

Todd's phone chimed with a message from Terry requesting a ride before the funeral, and he quickly replied with an affirmative "Yes." But before he could fully attend to the message, another call came in—from The Mexican.

Todd's heart seemed to freeze for a few moments, and a drop of cold sweat began to trickle down his forehead. He silenced the call with a sigh, his expression tense with apprehension. It was time to close the deal.

"Hum... For the payment..." Todd began, his attention returning to Ozzy.

"Oh yeah, yeah!" the lawyer replied eagerly, retrieving an envelope filled with cash from his luxury car and handing it over to Todd. The bills were crisp and new. "Here's the cash ya asked for!" Ozzy declared, a sense of satisfaction evident in his voice. He chuckled to himself, his laugh reminiscent of a hyena's cackle.

Todd nodded gratefully as he pocketed the envelope, his gaze lingering on the cottage for a moment longer. There was a heaviness in the air as if the woods themselves held their breath in anticipation.

The lawyer took the opportunity to say his final words: "You can come by to sign the documents whenever you want. You mentioned it was urgent, but I haven't had the time to prepare them yet."

"Okay. Sorry man, I gotta go. I got a funeral to get to," Todd apologized, his tone heavy with fake regret.

"Oh yeah, I heard about it... poor ol' Barney! My condolences, Todd!" Ozzy offered sympathetically as the mayor made his departure.

As Todd walked away, the lawyer returned to admire his new

purchase, his excitement palpable. He rubbed his hands together greedily, already imagining the profits he would reap from this venture… or maybe he wanted to keep it. Doubt flickered in Todd's eyes for a moment without knowing that someone was scrutinizing him.

On a nearby promontory, the detectives stood, observing the mayor's every move through binoculars, their expressions serious and focused. Kevin's gaze was steely, his mind already racing with theories and suspicions. "Looks like he sold the cottage," he remarked, his voice low yet distinct. There was a grim finality to his words, as if he knew that this sale marked the beginning of something far more sinister.

"He's lookin' for cash," James noted, his tone echoing his partner's concern. His eyes narrowed as he watched Ozzy's movements with suspicion.

"The question is: Why?" Kevin pondered aloud, his gaze fixed on Todd's departing figure.

"We'll figure it out soon enough," his partner reassured him, his resolve unwavering as Todd drove off into the distance, leaving behind a cloud of uncertainty.

A few hours later, at the cemetery, a somber gathering of mourners assembled for Barney's funeral. A small group of people, no more than ten in total, gathered around a freshly dug grave, their faces etched with grief and solemnity… no… just boredom.

Sure, funerals are no joyride, but upon closer inspection, no one seemed to truly consider Barney's untimely demise a tragedy. Among the attendees stood Todd, framed in the binoculars of the two detectives. He appeared casually bored, attempting to stifle a yawn as his gaze fixed on the casket being lowered into the ground. As the priest began to speak, Todd's attention drifted to Terry, who was dressed, yet again, in elegant mourning attire. The priest's words echoed across the cemetery, a bittersweet tribute to Barney's life and the legacy he left behind.

"Dear friends and family," the priest's voice carried on the gentle breeze, "today we have come together to honor the life of Barney. We have witnessed the challenges he faced, and triumphs he celebrated during his lifetime, and we were fortunate to have known and loved him. Although our hearts are heavy with his loss, we are here to celebrate his life and remember him with love."

Barney's wife stood among the mourners, her lack of grief evident as she absently tried to remove a stain from her dress. Todd's gaze lingered on her for a moment, noting her restless movements and impatient demeanor.

"As a community of faith," the priest continued, "we cling to the Christian hope of resurrection and eternal life, and we believe that Barney is now with the Lord in a place without pain or suffering. We pray that his soul may find peace and rest." Todd tried to focus on the priest's words, but his thoughts were elsewhere, on unanswered questions that lingered in his mind. "I would like to invite y'all to hold on to the good memories, move forward, and find comfort in your faith. May the Lord bless you and accompany you on your journey. Amen."

As the priest's farewell echoed through the cemetery, the mourners stood up almost immediately. No one wanted to spend a single second more than necessary there.

Only Todd was lost in thought. The cemetery around him emptied, but Terry, noticing his solitude and distress, went to take his hand to comfort him.

Todd embraced the woman affectionately, perhaps too affectionately.

James lowered the binoculars and observed his colleague's expression, but said nothing.

After the funeral, Todd and Terry left the cemetery to grab a bite to eat together, both unaware that they were being followed by the detectives. Thus, they managed to enjoy a pleasant evening despite the somber event that brought them together, staying together until dinner time, in a cozy and hospitable tavern.

The room was illuminated by the soft glow of sunset, a quiet refuge from the outside world. Todd and Terry sat at a table, their funeral attire still clinging to them like a shroud of grief. Todd's hands moved mechanically, slicing through the meat on his plate, his restless demeanor betraying the turmoil within. Terry watched him closely, her gaze lingering on his hands gripping the knife with an intensity that caught her attention. "Are you okay?" she ventured, her voice soft with concern.

Todd looked up, his eyes meeting hers with a mixture of surprise and gratitude. "Yeah. I'm okay," he replied, his voice tinged with a hint of uncertainty.

Terry sensed his unease and pressed further. "I see you actin' kinda weird. Is it 'cause of Barney?"

Todd shook his head, a faint smile tugging at the corners of his lips. "No. No, I mean… I didn't actually expect you to have dinner with me," he admitted, his words weighted with emotion. "It almost doesn't seem real to be able to spend such a nice time with you, despite the circumstances."

Terry reached out her hand, finding his in a gesture of comfort. "I sensed that your soul needed me. I'm very sensitive to these kinds of things," she murmured.

Todd's gaze softened as he returned her touch, his eyes locking with hers in an intense moment of connection. "Do you wanna stay with me tonight?" he asked, his voice barely above a whisper.

Terry's breath caught in her throat, a blush rising to her cheeks as she lowered her gaze shyly. "I remind you that you have a wife at home waitin' for you," she replied, her words tinged with uncertainty.

Todd shook his head, his resolve unwavering. "She won't be home 'cause she's on the night shift... and besides, I don't need just anyone, I need you... and I want you," he confessed, his words hanging in the air between them.

Terry was taken aback by his honesty, her heart fluttering in her chest at the sincerity of his words.

A moment of silence stretched between them. Sensing the need to break the tension, Terry spoke up. "I'll come over tonight. Just gotta take care of somethin' and then I'll be right there with ya," she said, a smile playing at the corners of her lips as she raised her glass of wine. There was a flutter of excitement in her chest.

"Yeah, I gotta sort out a matter myself before anything else… so let's go?" In a few minutes, the two lovebirds left the tavern, and as agreed, Todd accompanied Terry to her apartment.

The only thing that had changed outside was the weather; it was raining, and the two detectives were sitting in their car with the windows fogged up as their surveillance resumed. Rain poured down relentlessly, casting a somber veil over the night as Todd's car pulled up outside Terry's apartment. With hurried steps, Terry dashed from the car to the shelter of her building, fumbling with her keys as she hastened to unlock the door.

In the distance, the detectives' car approached, its lights dimmed to conceal its presence as it parked a half mile behind Todd's vehicle.

Inside the detective's car, confusion clouded their expressions as they observed Todd's actions.

"So... it's just a booty call," said Reyes, his sad smile almost breaking through.

Kevin's disappointment was palpable as he processed the situation. "C'mon, he's headin' out!" he exclaimed, determination creeping into his tone.

As Todd's car pulled away, the detectives followed cautiously, maintaining a discreet distance to avoid detection.

"Give 'im some room, so we don't git caught!" Sun instructed as they trailed behind Todd, who kept driving and didn't even stop when Marfa was far behind him.

The detectives could follow Todd from a distance thanks to the GPS, but they certainly didn't expect to spend a rough night out in the middle of the desert. Their car sliced through the darkness, its headlights casting eerie shadows on the rain-soaked terrain. The partners navigated the desolate landscape, their eyes fixed on the GPS tracking their target's movements.

"Where the hell are we headed?" Kevin grumbled, his frustration growing with each passing mile.

"I reckon we're gettin' close to the border," James replied, his attention split between the road ahead and the digital map on his phone.

As they continued their pursuit, James glanced back at the screen. "Looks like he pulled over by an old mine," he reported, his voice tinged with anticipation.

Kevin surveyed their surroundings, a sense of déjà vu settling over him.

"If memory serves, this is the same road where Barney met his end, ain't it?" he mused aloud.

"It appears that the sheriff's workin' theory that 'this road didn't lead nowhere...' was wrong," James remarked dryly, a hint of skepticism in his tone.

With a heavy sigh, Kevin pulled out his gun for a brief check.

"Haven't used this in at least ten years."

"You've been lucky then," James replied.

"Let's hope my luck holds out."

THE MEXICAN

RAIN POURED DOWN in torrents, obscuring the abandoned mine nestled within the desolate landscape. Light flickered from the windows of an old log cabin, casting eerie shadows on the rain-soaked ground where Todd's car, alongside other vehicles, including a van, was parked outside.

From the cover of darkness, the detectives approached stealthily, walking cautiously through the ankle-deep mud as they surveyed the scene before them. "Probably nearly in Mexico by now," Kevin whispered, his voice barely audible above the sound of the rain.

"Yeah, what the devil do ya think is goin' on?" the partner replied, his tone worried.

Kevin swiftly snapped a picture with his phone before turning to his companion. "Let's check it out," he suggested, determination etched in his face.

The detectives crept closer to the cabin, their senses alert as they approached a crack in the wood, through which they could glimpse inside, being careful not to make any noise that might betray their presence.

The glow of a television illuminated the faces of the detectives as they peered through the crack, the sound of a football game emanating from within.

Inside the cabin, Todd stood facing The Mexican—the detectives seeing him for the first time—a man of short stature with a dark and menacing appearance. He was undoubtedly a member of the Mexican cartel, as evidenced by his horrendous, outdated shirt, as well as the piles of drugs scattered everywhere. The man seemed tense, his gaze unwavering as he awaited some kind of response from Todd.

With a cigar clutched between his fingers, he lounged in his makeshift "office", surrounded by drugs and cash, and flanked by two armed guards who remained vigilant.

The cartel leader swiftly counted some banknotes with a machine. When he observed the amount, he commented with a disdainful look towards Todd, "This money ain't coverin' the whole thing, but... it'll do for now." He casually pocketed the envelope of cash and offered Todd a couple of bricks of cocaine.

The mayor hesitated, his demeanor tense, and after a long silence, he spoke like a timid student to the teacher. "Did ya take out my buddies?" he questioned, his voice edged with accusation.

The Mexican exchanged a meaningful glance with his men before replying, "I've killed many people. You should be more specific." His tone was laced with menace, though he ended the sentence with a proud smile—a reaction to his men's laughter. Suddenly, however, The Mexican became serious again, scrutinizing Todd as he stood.

As tension hung heavy in the air, The Mexican motioned to his men, who lowered the volume of the TV, amplifying the gravity of the moment.

Outside, the detectives observed the exchange with bated breath, their expressions mirroring the intensity of the scene unfolding before them.

Todd's resolve hardened as he seized the bricks of cocaine and stuffed them into a bag. "You know what? I don't give a damn," he declared defiantly, his words echoing through the room.

The Mexican's reaction was swift as he bellowed a command to his men, his anger palpable. "Beto!" he called out, prompting the arrival of a tough-looking man accompanied by a young girl—little more than a child—who bore evident signs of injuries and mistreatment.

James observed the almost lifeless girl, and his gaze hardened, becoming unreadable even to Kevin.

Rain continued to pour relentlessly as the detectives observed the scene from their concealed vantage point. Instinctively, James slowly reached for his gun, but his partner intervened with a hand, his voice barely above a whisper. "Hold yer horses, cowboy! We're outnumbered, and they're packin' some serious heat! Didn't you see all those automatics?!" Kevin cautioned, his tone urgent.

Indeed, James hadn't noticed, but practically everyone in the cabin was armed, even though they appeared relaxed while watching the game.

James, though visibly nervous, had no other choice and reluctantly complied, keeping his hand away from his weapon as they continued to observe in silence.

The Mexican regarded Todd with an almost amused expression, his intent clear as he sought to provoke a reaction. "My men are tired of her. She bites and doesn't talk... What am I supposed to do about this girl?" he queried, his voice tinged with irritation.

Todd sighed wearily, his patience wearing thin as he contemplated his next move. "You do you! I'm hightailin' it outta here!" the mayor retorted, his resolve unwavering despite the escalating tension.

But The Mexican wasn't finished yet, a sly smirk playing across his lips as he issued his command. "Hold on! Bring her to Bob, he'll show her a good time," The Mexican suggested, his tone dripping with sinister intent.

Todd balked at the suggestion, his expression hardening with resolve.

"Bob don't roll that way," Todd countered defiantly.

The conversation about the girl's fate grew increasingly unclear to the detectives. What was certain though, was that The Mexican was holding onto her for Todd, who no longer wanted her back and couldn't care less about her fate. The partners exchanged confused glances, struggling to make sense of the situation. James silently mouthed a question to his partner, who could only offer a shrug in response. "Who the hell is Bob?".

As Todd gathered his belongings and made his exit, the detectives remained concealed, snapping pictures as he drove off into the night. James, his determination unwavering, voiced his resolve. "We'll grab him later. We gotta save the girl!" His gaze was intense as he checked his weapon for readiness.

Kevin, though initially hesitant, ultimately nodded in agreement, recognizing the urgency of the situation. "Hang tight here, I'm callin' in backup from the ride!" Kevin instructed, his voice firm as he left the porch, careful not to make any noise.

"What a magical synchronicity that on that very night, they were playing Janis Joplin on the radio…"

The haunting melody of Janis Joplin's "Ball and Chain" echoed softly, filling the space with its soulful rhythm. As Terry meticulously applied her makeup, the radio crooned lazily in the background. A strange sense of unease seemed to grip Terry's soul, causing her to pause for a moment of contemplation, but the song started playing again like nothing happened, and soon enough, the easy vibe filled the room once more.

Dressed in nothing but lingerie and a garter belt, Terry stole a glance at the clock before succumbing to the music's intoxicating allure. She rose to her feet and began to dance in front of the mirror. With each sway of her hips, she exuded a magnetic sensuality, lost in the rhythm of the song. It was almost time; she needed to calm down.

Meanwhile, Todd was on his way back to her apartment, as agreed, navigating the dark deserted roads. His car sliced through the darkness like a solitary vessel adrift in the sea. Casting a wary glance at the rearview mirror, Todd's senses were heightened, a silent vigilance etched into his features as he pressed on into the night. He couldn't be certain, but he felt something was wrong on that damn night. However, things would soon be sorted out.

He couldn't wait to be alone with Terry; he enjoyed this latest fling because, in a way, it proved to him that, despite the years, he could still be a true conqueror... if he wanted.

Under the incessant rain, Kevin tried to contact reinforcements from the car. "Can you hear me, guys?"

"I can hear... not well." Their connection was disrupted by the bad weather. Keven tried everything to communicate quickly, but it wasn't possible.

Inside the cabin, the soccer game kept the men occupied, but it was nearing its end, and James began to fear the worst. The Mexican and his men were discussing what to do after the game, and even though James couldn't hear perfectly what they were saying, he only had to use his imagination. They wanted to get rid of the girl.

In the flickering glow of the television, The Mexican passed a machete to his henchman with chilling nonchalance. The tension mounted as he issued his ominous command. "Get rid of the girl. Cut off her head and throw the body into the mine."

James' entire nervous system snapped into a state of rage so intense that he only thought, "I don't care if I die now, but I'm taking these bastards to Hell with me!" His clarity turned into anger, resentment, and personal vendetta. His hand was already on his gun, although he didn't realize it immediately.

Then, with three sharp whistle blows, the scene erupted into chaos. Reyes burst into the room, his gun drawn as he commanded authority over the stunned occupants. "You're all under arrest, you sons of bitches!" He thundered, the door slamming behind him.

In a heartbeat, a standoff ensued, the air crackling with tension as each side weighed their next moves. Suddenly, the Mexicans reached for their weapons, and James began to take them down. Only one managed to grab a rifle and return fire, but James shot him in the foot from under the couch. As soon as he hit the ground, James hit him square in the temple.

The Mexican made a desperate escape bid, dragging the young girl with him, but the second door was locked, and Beto had bolted. The room erupted into a deadly dance of survival as The Mexican held the girl by the neck, and James took aim at him.

The detective was soaked through, sweat dripping from every part of him as the Mexican shouted at him, "Let me out or I'll kill her! I swear I'll slit this girl's throat because of you!"

"You're under arrest! You ain't goin' nowhere, and if you harm that girl, I'll shove this gun up your ass and empty it inside you!" James responded. The detective was Mexican-borne, and he knew the cartel members well. He knew they were beasts of the worst kind and that it was pointless to negotiate with them. Driven by rage, James struggled to remain clear-headed as the two circled the room. Blood started to seep from James's arm. He had been hit without even realizing it, but fortunately, it was just a graze. A Mexican standoff ensued as the cartel boss tried to reach the exit, and after a while, he succeeded. James couldn't do anything; shooting would endanger the girl being used as a shield, and that son of a bitch was exactly as tall as she was.

With the door behind him, the Mexican warned, "I'm leaving, and if I see you following me, I'll kill her!"

In a swift and decisive move, Detective Sun stepped out from beyond the door and, aiming his gun high, fired a shot into the back of The Mexican's head. The cartel leader fell to the ground, dragging the girl with him, a permanent look of disbelief on his face. The girl, clearly terrified, began to huddle up and mumble something through her sobs.

It seemed like it was over; the tension dropped from a thousand to zero in a second, and that's when James was reminded that he had a hole in his arm. It didn't seem too serious, but he slumped for a moment at the sight of the blood seeping out. Kevin steadied him, reassuring him, "Reinforcements are on the way. I told them to bring an ambulance." With the threat extinguished, the night reclaimed its silence.

LOVE IS BLIND

IN TERRY'S APARTMENT, everything seemed poised for a steamy rendezvous. The doorbell chimed eagerly, prompting Terry's heart to quicken its pace. With measured steps, she approached the door, anticipation coursing through her veins. Swinging it open, she was met by Todd's commanding presence, his aura filling the room with an intensity that sent shivers down her spine. His eyes lingered on her figure, adorned in a sheer nightgown and provocative lingerie, igniting a fiery desire that crackled in the air between them.

Without a word, Todd crossed the threshold, the door slamming shut behind him as he pulled Terry into his arms with a hunger that bordered on desperation. As they began to undress, passion ignited, fulfilling a longing they had both harbored for far too long.

Todd surrendered to a night of uninhibited passion while outside the city, at the abandoned mine, he had left behind a significant debt that was about to engulf him.

James cradled the sobbing young girl in his arms, his heart heavy with the weight of her pain. As her tears flowed freely, he whispered words of comfort in Spanish. Detective Sun lit a cigarette, the glowing ember casting a dim light on the grim scene behind him in the cabin.

With reinforcements on the way and ambulances en route, the promise of aid offered a glimmer of hope amidst the darkness, accompanied by the wail of approaching sirens.

Suddenly, a series of thuds reverberated from one of the parked vans, drawing the detectives' attention. "What was that?" James asked.

With cautious steps, Kevin approached the vehicle, his hand gripping his gun tightly as he prepared for the worst. Opening the van, he was met with a sight that chilled him to the core—six immigrants, their faces etched with exhaustion and fear, huddled together in the cramped space.

They were prisoners and they were desperate.

The detective was shocked to see humans treated that way and hurried to get them out of the van, providing them with first aid. The night erupted into a symphony of flashing lights and blaring sirens, the arrival of police cars, DEA agents, and ambulances heralding the dawn of a new chapter in the unfolding drama. James received medical attention, but his condition was not serious. Turning to his partner, Detective Sun offered a silent nod of solidarity, their resolve unwavering in the face of adversity.

In a fleeting moment of tenderness, the young girl broke free from the doctor's grasp, her trembling form seeking solace in James' arms once more. As he held her close, a sense of purpose washed over him. The two detectives exchanged another glance and nodded, their faces reflecting the determination to close this chapter once and for all.

"And so, it was finally game over…"

In the dimly lit bedroom of Terry's apartment, Todd lay asleep, his snores filling the quiet space with a rhythmic hum. Suddenly, heavy knocks echoed through the room, jolting him awake. Confusion clouded his mind as he struggled to grasp the reality of the situation. Rubbing his eyes, he noticed blood staining his hand. His gaze shifted to Terry, lying motionless on the bed, a pool of blood surrounding her.

"What the fuck!?" Shock coursed through Todd as he realized the gravity of the situation before him.

Meanwhile, from outside, screams began to echo. "Open the door! Mr. Mayor, we know you're inside!"

Beside Terry's lifeless form lay a knife, its gleaming blade catching the light in Todd's hands as he found himself holding it, swiftly pulling it away. Panic surged within him as the pounding against the door intensified, the voices of the detectives and police officers growing louder with each passing moment.

"Todd, open up! We know you're in there!"

With trembling hands, Todd grasped the knife, his mind racing with disbelief and fear. Clad only in his underwear, he stood frozen in place, desperate to find a solution. But the relentless demands of the law bore down upon him, urging him to relinquish the weapon and face the harsh reality of his circumstances.

As the detectives and police officers breached the door, flashlights and guns drawn, Todd's heart pounded in his chest, his every instinct screaming for survival. Terry's body was there, incriminating him, and he had the murder weapon right in his hand. Facing the first officers who were blinding him with their flashlights and shouting at him, he cried out in desperation, "It wasn't me! I've been framed!" Yet amidst the chaos, his protestations fell on deaf ears, and he seemed unaware of himself shouting something.

"Drop the weapon!" yelled Kevin.

James followed up. "Drop the knife! Don't do anything stupid!"

In a moment of sheer desperation, Todd's resolve shattered, and he lunged forward, his vision clouded by rage and confusion. The sharp crack of gunfire pierced the air as James's bullet found its mark, sending Todd crashing to the ground, his body wracked with pain, his consciousness fading.

And so, amidst the shadows of betrayal and deceit, Todd's world crumbled around him, destroyed by the cruel hands of fate. As darkness closed in, the echoes of his anguished cries reverberated through the room. "It wasn't me! I have been framed!"

"Yeah Todd, they framed you, but you ain't innocent, are ya?"

The street outside Terry's apartment was teeming with onlookers, drawn by the flashing lights of police cars and the wail of ambulance sirens. Police officers worked to disperse the curious crowd, urging them to clear the area and allow the authorities to do their work.

The spectators already knew something was up.

"Did you hear?! They got the mayor!"

"No, he's not dead, just injured!"

"Damn cops with their heavy-handed tactics!"

"But are we sure he's innocent?!"

"Ladies and gentlemen, please step back—police operation in progress!" shouted one of the officers, eyeing Terry's apartment where the door was already wide open, emitting dozens of camera flashes.

Amidst the commotion, the detectives stood quietly, their gazes fixed on the crime scene before them. Todd, pale and unconscious, was wheeled out on a stretcher, an IV drip trailing behind him. The ambulance whisked him away into the night, leaving behind a trail of unanswered questions.

The apartment superintendent hovered nearby, a silent witness to the unfolding drama, alongside a cluster of curious teenagers who should have been home long ago. "Hey, kids! Go home! This isn't a place for you!" barked the old man, eliciting laughter from the youths near him who withdrew nonetheless.

Kevin's brow furrowed in deep concentration as he pondered the tangled web of mysteries surrounding the events of the night. The detectives followed Todd's stretcher for a few steps and then stopped to talk as he was loaded into the ambulance. The bastard was still alive.

"I'm hopin' he pulls through long enough for me to put two and two together. This story has a lot of holes in it," Kevin murmured, his voice tinged with determination.

James nodded in agreement, his expression grim. "Even if he bites the dust, ain't no one gonna cry over it."

"But I gotta know who that Mexican was goin' on about—they mentioned 'Bob'," Sun continued, his tone resolute.

Reyes nodded thoughtfully.

"I recall, but that's why we're in a pickle—lots'a Bobs 'round these parts."

"We need to find him!" Kevin declared, his eyes flashing with determination. With purposeful strides, he approached the entrance of Terry's apartment, where camera flashes illuminated the darkened doorway. James followed closely behind, his resolve unwavering in the face of uncertainty.

"Well, at least this time they've beefed-up our staffing, thank the Lord," Reyes remarked, a faint glimmer of optimism amidst the chaos.

"Only 'cause Todd was a bigger fish than he seemed."

The two detectives re-entered the apartment, their attention focused on the latest victim, Terry. Her lifeless body lay sprawled on the bed, her vacant stare hauntingly illuminated by the harsh flash of forensic cameras.

A forensic officer approached the detectives and began to comment on the scene and the case. "The preliminary examination indicates that the victim has a penetrating wound to the neck that is sharp and precise, suggesting intentional criminal action," he remarked, his voice carrying a somber weight as he documented the grim scene.

The bed was a canvas of crimson, soaked with the evidence of violence. Another flash illuminated the chilling tableau, casting stark shadows across the room. A knife lay discarded on the floor, its blade stained with blood. The forensic team meticulously combed through the apartment, scrutinizing every detail for clues, while the detectives observed from a respectful distance just beyond the threshold.

James, visibly shaken by the grisly sight, broke the heavy silence. "Let's get out of here. I've had enough blood for tonight," he muttered, his voice heavy with the weight of the evening's horrors. With a heavy sigh, Kevin nodded in agreement, silently following his partner and leaving behind the crime scene.

ANOTHER... 'VICTIM'

IN THE EARLY morning light, the detectives found themselves parked at a roadside restaurant along the Texas plains. Kevin leaned against the hood of their car, his gaze fixed on the vast expanse of the landscape before him. Meanwhile, James stood nearby, engaged in a phone call as he ordered coffee.

"Alright! Much obliged, y'all!" Reyes said into the phone before ending the call and handing a cup of coffee to his partner. "They located the gal's folks," James began, "they figured she'd taken off from home. Her pa was Todd's political opponent in the last go-round. Everyone else is good to go."

Kevin nodded, but his mind seemed elsewhere. A long, introspective silence settled in the car between the two. "Todd asked The Mexican if he offed his buddies," the older detective said.

"And?" inquired James.

"That there means ol' Todd didn't kill 'em."

"Maybe not. Maybe the Mexican did it," Reyes suggested, adding, "or maybe he knew we were listening..." He stretched and yawned; he was exhausted.

"Okay. So... why kill the woman?"

Between yawns, James managed to mumble a response.

"Maybe she stumbled onto somethin'? Maybe she tried to put a stop to it? But we'll never know for sure 'less he pulls through and we can ask 'im. But from such an animal... I certainly don't expect the truth." James punctuated his words with a piercing gaze.

"Somethin's mighty peculiar here, partner. We've gone an' unlocked Pandora's box—the further we dig, the more trouble we find," remarked Kevin.

With a tired yawn, Reyes suggested, "Okay but... let's hit the hay. It's been a long night."

Sun nodded, placed his hands on the steering wheel, started the engine, and they both drove off, leaving behind unresolved questions.

"Them two detectives were real sharp, you know? Ah... nowadays, you just don't find folks of that caliber around no more..."

The same afternoon, after resting for a few hours, the detectives made their way to the hospital where Todd had been taken. Ironically, he lay unaware in the same bed that Daly had lain in when he had tried to kill her.

A mechanical ventilator hummed softly, providing life-sustaining breaths. The steady beep of an electrocardiogram punctuated the room's quiet tension.

Kevin stood at the door, peering in at Todd's motionless form with a contemplative expression. James joined him, bringing news, their eyes fixed on Todd's unconscious figure through the glass. "They said the bullet did some damage to his aorta, but he made it." His voice tinged with a mixture of relief and indifference. "He's out cold for now, thanks to all those meds they pumped into him. Even if it turns out I'm the one who took him down, I ain't losin' any sleep over it."

Kevin turned to his partner, gratitude evident in his gaze. "And you shouldn't... You saved our lives. That idiot was armed with a knife!"

There was a moment of silence.

"I always got yer back," James reassured him, his tone firm.

Kevin's thoughts drifted, pondering the uncertain fate of Todd's wife. "Wonder what's gonna happen to his missus..." he mused aloud, his voice trailing off as they exchange a knowing look. "Strange that the lovely wife ain't by her husband's side right now, don't you think?"

"Yeah, real strange... Let's go!"

YEAH! LET'S GO!

TODD'S HOUSE STOOD with its front door wide open. The trunk of Cindy's car gaped open as well. Under the scorching Texas sun, the sheriff hurriedly packs boxes into her car, her movements tense and jittery. The detectives arrived unexpectedly, their sudden appearance startling her.

"Hey, Sheriff! You skedaddlin'?" Kevin called out casually, a hint of suspicion in his tone.

Cindy stammered, caught off guard by their presence. "Oh! Detectives! No. I.. I.."

"Looks like yer skippin' town, ma'am," James interjected, his eyes narrowing as he surveyed the scene.

The woman stared at the two detectives for a long moment, trying to calm herself. She was agitated, and it was all too evident. Even her cheeks were flushed. She tried to appear calm, but she simply couldn't.

"No foolin' Cindy, a missus who ain't standin' by her man right now is suspicious, if you catch my drift," Kevin asserted, his voice low and probing.

Cindy inhaled sharply, her eyes darting nervously between the detectives.

"He was steppin' out on me!" she blurted out, her frustration evident but forced.

"Were you privy to any of his secrets?" the detective pressed, his gaze piercing.

Cindy hesitated, struggling to compose herself.

"You know he was workin' with a Cartel? Maybe you even helped him… that would explain why you're in such a hurry, am I right?" Reyes cut in, his tone resolute.

Cindy attempted to regain her composure. "A wife can't testify against her husband, right?" she asked weakly, her voice tinged with uncertainty.

"So, you knew!" James had to struggle to hold himself back, and his partner stopped him with an arm.

There was a long silence.

Kevin leaned in, his expression serious. "Cindy, there's a few things that ain't addin' up here. Why don't you give us a hand… and we'll look the other way?"

Cindy took a moment to respond, but with her back against the wall, she slowly nodded, her resolve solidifying as she took a deep breath.

"What can I do for you, Detective?" she asked, steeling herself.

"I'll take everythin' you know, but first things first… who exactly is Bob?" Kevin demanded.

Cindy hesitated, a look of "obviousness" painted on her face.

"Yeah, who's Bob? Y'all remember him? It's tough 'cause, you see… he'd spent his whole life stayin' outta sight…"

"Dang son of a bitch!" Kevin exclaimed, yanking the brake sharply.

The detectives pulled up to the police station in their car, tires squealing as they hastily parked. The two hurriedly made their way inside, talking to each other in an agitated manner. "How in tarnation didn' we catch on to it sooner!"

As they entered, some cops waved in greeting, but the detectives pressed on.

Spotting them, the forensics officer from Terry's scene approached with a sheet in hand. His name for the first time recognizable from the badge on his chest: George. "Oh, Detectives!" he called out, trying to catch their attention.

"Hold your horses, George! Your name's George?!" Kevin snapped.

"Yeah," the officer nodded blankly, showing the badge.

"We're on the lookout for Bob!" the detective continued urgently.

"Bob? He's not here, I don't think he's on shift today," George informed them. The detectives paused, exchanging a glance before turning their gazes back to the forensic expert. "I was just about to bring y'all up to speed. These here are the results from the latest autopsy. I got all of Todd's phone data right here on the desk too." He handed over the sheet of paper. Kevin took the document, his interest piqued. "I think somethin' ain't right. Look carefully!" George urged, sensing their confusion.

Kevin quickly scanned the document, his expression shifting as he processed the information. He then handed it to James, who read it with growing disbelief. "Are you pullin' my leg?" Reyes asked incredulously.

George was at a loss for words, his confusion palpable.

"No. I... I..." he stammered, unable to explain.

But Detective Sun intervened, raising a hand to halt his stumbling words. "One thing at a time..." he interjected, his mind already racing with new possibilities. Turning to his partner, the detective nodded decisively.

"Let's go…" he said, leading the way out of the police station.

As they departed, George remained standing there, still processing the strange interaction.

"Hey Bob, they're comin' for ya…"

As the detectives' car cruised down a desolate country road, the setting sun cast long shadows over the rugged landscape, and the atmosphere inside the car was tense. Behind the wheel, Kevin steered steadily, his gaze fixed on the winding road ahead. Beside him, his partner appeared tense, lost in contemplation. Finally, James' voice cut through the uneasy silence. "You think we're nearing the end of this tale?"

Kevin sighed, his eyes reflecting a mix of determination and weariness. "There's only one way to find out. Seems like it's all intertwined somehow. Points to the fact that justice 'round these parts ain't been up to snuff."

Lost in memories, Reyes' expression softened, his gaze drifting to the passing scenery. "For me, it's hard not to take it personally… being an immigrant myself," he mused. "Seein' those folks crammed in that van… it brings back some painful memories." His voice trembled as he recounted the harrowing experience. "I can still see it, clear as day… We were packed in like sardines, just like them. Then the van caught fire… People were panicking, kids trampled… My old man tried to shield me, but…" He trailed off, the memories still vivid in his mind.

Kevin listened attentively, attempting to understand the weight of his partner's past. "I get it," he said softly, adding, "But we can't afford to let emotions cloud our judgment right now. If Bob's even half as dangerous as Cindy claims, we gotta stay sharp."

Reyes nodded, a steely resolve flickering in his eyes. In a matter of minutes, the detectives' car pulled up in front of Bob's house.

"It must be this one, if I got it right," said James.

A solitary structure stood engulfed by the encroaching shadows of the fading sun. Its facade was weathered, with peeling paint and broken shutters. "Obviously, this is the one," said Sun, looking at the house that seemed straight out of a Tim Burton movie. The overgrown yard, tangled with weeds and littered with debris, spoke of years of neglect and solitude. A creaky porch, with missing floorboards and a dilapidated swing, added to the eerie atmosphere, making the house seem like a forgotten relic haunted by its past.

Inside the house, Bob moved like a ghost against the backdrop of a flickering stove. Shadows danced on the walls as the dim light from the burners cast an eerie glow over the somber, vintage 1950s decor.

The officer's bare torso bore a Confederate flag tattoo, a symbol of love for his rugged past. The sudden chime of the doorbell pierced the air, catching him off guard. Bob quickly threw on a shirt and grabbed a remote control to turn up the volume on the television. With measured steps, he approached the door, concealing the unease gnawing at him.

As Bob swung open the door, he was met by the steely gaze of the detectives, their presence ominous. Tension crackled in the air as they exchanged pleasantries, veiled threats lurking beneath the surface. "Hey, Bob!" Kevin greeted him cheerfully. "We just wanted to ask you a few questions…" The off-duty officer was taken aback, clearly not expecting visitors.

"Y'all ain't gonna invite us in?" James cut in, his face twisted into a menacing grin.

With a reluctant nod, Bob allowed them entry, the creak of the door sounding like a portent of doom. The detectives' footsteps began to creak on the old floorboards. But the sound didn't bother them, as the only noise that truly filled the air came from the television in the kitchen. The partners searched the house, their eyes hungry for truth amidst the facade of normalcy. Old photographs adorned the walls, capturing moments of triumph during domestic life. Among the photos of Bob as a child was one with his long-deceased mother, looking as unsettling as a horror movie witch.

James' attention to the portrait seemed to unsettle Bob, who asked,

"So, what do y'all wanna ask me?"

Sweat glistened on his brow, betraying his inner turmoil.

Kevin observed the sweat and spoke in a deliberately ambiguous manner. "So, you had time to clean up, huh?"

Bob's heart skipped a beat, but Kevin ran a finger over a piece of furniture to indicate he was referring to the dust. The officer smiled weakly and mumbled something about having a cleaning lady. His words trailed off as his unease grew.

Suddenly, beneath the booming sound of the loud television, James heard a noise—a strange, rough, vibrating crescendo, like something being dragged into the next room.

"What was that?" James asked, his detective senses tingling. He listened carefully, picking up something, then immediately went to the television and turned it off.

Bob only had time to stiffen and put on the look of a child being punished. A discordant symphony of sound enveloped the room, the metallic clinking echoing like the toll of a funeral bell. With a sense of foreboding, Kevin uncovered a hidden trapdoor concealed beneath the corridor's worn carpet. The two detectives exchanged a glance, and James nodded as Bob shrank into himself. "You need a warrant! Come back when..."

James took his gun in hand saying, "Here's my warrant! Now shut up and open this damn door!"

Bob raised his hands and, though reluctant, did as he was told. He opened the trapdoor using a key he kept in his pocket. A heavy darkness filled the basement as Detective Sun cautiously descended the stairs. The overwhelming stench of decay assaulted his senses. "Damn, it sure does reek in here! James keep an eye on him while I take a look around." Switching on his flashlight, the detective's beam revealed a long chain snaking down the stairs. With measured steps, he followed its path, the cold metal railing biting into his palm. "I think there's a dog down here! God, it stinks!"

"Watch out for the dog! It might be trained and violent!" James suggested from above.

The detective grabbed his gun and continued to explore deeper into the basement. He just kept following the long chain that trembled as it disappeared into the darkness.

Suddenly, the light fell upon a disheveled little girl, shackled behind a bookshelf. Her dark eyes, wide with terror, bore into his soul, pleading for salvation.

"For the love of God!" The detective's voice reverberated through the darkness as he called out to his partner. "James! There's a girl down here! Turn on the lights!"

The detective's urgent command echoed through the house, but before his partner could respond, Bob seized the opportunity to strike. A scuffle broke out, but unfortunately for Bob, James was damn strong and well-trained, unlike his usual victims.

A flurry of blows ensued as they grappled for control of the gun, which clattered to the ground in their struggle.

Soon James found himself dominating the situation despite the wound on his arm. His greatest challenge was to contain his anger.

James shouted down through the open trapdoor to respond to his colleague. "Gimme a minute, will ya? I'm almost done!" With steely determination, James wrested back control, his hands trembling as he pointed the weapon. "I ain't no helpless little girl, Bob. Now turn on them damn lights!" James punctuated his command with a fierce headbutt to Bob's nose, breaking it.

"Ah, you no-good son of a bitch! You busted my nose!"

"Thank God and all your muertos that I'm stoppin' there!"

The crack of the gun punctuated his demand as Bob cowered under the force of his authority.

Meanwhile, in the basement, Kevin extended a calming hand, but the girl recoiled in terror, her chains rattling against the cold concrete floor. "Hey, calm down! I ain't gonna hurt you none!"

With a desperate cry, the little girl fled into the darkness, dragging her chains in her wake.

As neon lights flickered to life, the basement was bathed in an eerie glow, revealing its sinister secrets. Rows of VHS tapes lined the shelves, their labels obscured by layers of dust and grime. Pornographic posters leered from the walls, their lurid imagery stained with blood.

In the center of the room lay a sordid tableau—a filthy bed, adorned with a tripod and camera, a grotesque scene for unspeakable horrors.

Forcing Bob down the stairs at gunpoint, Reyes confronted him with righteous fury.

"Move it, motherfucker!"

Bob's broken nose oozed blood as he stumbled forward, his eyes ablaze with fear. James' gun pressed into his back, urging him toward his reckoning.

A few minutes later, Bob was bound to a chair with duct tape, his defiant demeanor wavering in the face of impending retribution. "You can't do this to me! I'm sick!"

"You bet your ass you're sick. Where them keys at?"

Kevin's voice dripped with disdain as he aimed the gun at Bob's face. "Don't make me say it twice!"

With a sneer, Bob revealed the location of the keys, a twisted grin dancing across his lips. "The keys're in ma wallet, which's in ma pocket." The detective retrieved the wallet, his grip tightening on the gun as Bob taunted him once more. "Now that y'all had yer moment of glory, I'd like to kindly ask y'all to arrest me and end this damn circus."

With a silent nod, Kevin passed the keys to his partner, who moved to release the captive girl.

As James approached the trembling child, Kevin's gaze fell upon a sinister black garbage bag in the shadows.

Steeling himself against the putrid stench, the detective unearthed a grisly truth: the lifeless body of another innocent girl.

Bob's mocking laughter pierced the suffocating air, a grotesque echo of his depravity. "What's the matter, detective? Ain't got the stomach for it?"

James was able to free the little girl and asked, "What is it?" His concern was palpable as he turned to the detective, who stood transfixed by the grim discovery. Silent tears betrayed the detective's anguish as he stepped away from the bag, his resolve hardening with each passing moment.

With a trembling voice, the little girl pointed to the bag and uttered a name: "Graciela", now consigned to the heavens. Sorrow washed over James as he gathered the now sobbing child in his arms, promising her safety and solace.

Bob watched the scene, clicking his tongue in his blood-filled mouth. "Well, ain't that just a heart-warmin' lil' scene." Kevin's steely glare cut through Bob's callous facade, his fists clenched with restrained fury. "What's the matter? Ya'll think ya got me shakin' in my boots?"

With a swift blow, Kevin unleashed his pent-up rage, and then a second time, each punch a point for the justice long overdue. Bob took the blows, remaining powerless, and immediately began to cry desperately.

"Alright Bob, now you oughtta let the cat outta the bag and tell me the whole damn truth. Everything you know... starting with the Daly Flores case. And if you don't talk, I'm gonna keep punching you until you spit out all your teeth. This ain't no joke, Bob."

KNOWING THIS...

DETECTIVE SUN EMERGED from the basement and noticed that it was now raining outside. His hand was stained with blood and throbbing with pain. His face bore splatters of blood as well. He considered washing his hands in the kitchen sink. James was there, taking care of the little girl.

As the detective approached the sink to rinse his aching hand, James' voice broke the silence, laden with concern.

"This little girl needs medical care and psychological support. I tried to sit her on the couch, but she won't let me." With a weary sigh, Kevin nodded in understanding, the weight of their grim task heavy upon him. "So? Did he spill the beans?"

Kevin nodded affirmatively, a glimmer of disbelief in his eyes.

"Yeah, he's tied up like a fresh salami in the chair now, awaitin' his fate. You ain't even gonna believe this! Bob was singin' like a canary! Even about Todd and all his buddies!"

James absorbed this revelation with a thoughtful nod, the little girl squirming in his arms, seeking solace. "What's the plan of action here?"

Kevin's gaze drifted out the window and into the distance, his mind consumed by the tangled web of deceit.

"I gotta head down to San Antonio to make sure of all this."

"Nah, I'm talkin' about Bob..." James clarified grimly.

Kevin's expression darkened, grappling with the weight of their failures. "Bob... We screwed things up."

A sense of bewilderment lingered in the air as James offered reassurance, cradling the now sleeping child in his arms.

"I'll take care of this... go ahead and take the girl to the car."

Kevin hesitated, torn between duty and a gnawing sense of unease.

"You sure about this? We can still turn 'round..."

With a resolute nod, James transferred the girl to his partner's arms, a silent promise echoing between them.

"Ain't likely. Go on now... take this gal to the car, and I'll handle it from here... I told you it was personal for me."

In the somber exchange of glances, a silent understanding passed between the detectives, a bond forged in the crucible of justice and vengeance.

Kevin did as he was told. He took the little girl and grabbed some snacks for her from the cupboard. Without saying another word, he left the house carrying the girl in his arms, who asked, "Can I have some candy?"

"The Lord'll deal with those two detectives when the time comes, but what would y'all have done?"

Bob's house was enveloped in silence.

James looked around, a strange sensation growing within him. He knew what he was about to do. Maybe it wasn't right, but damn it, he needed to clear his head for a moment.

That house reeked of dampness and socks. What a mess.

James stepped into the bathroom, facing his reflection in the mirror. He turned the taps on the sink, the sound of running water mingling with the distant rumble of thunder outside.

His hands gripped the edges of the sink, knuckles white with suppressed rage. "It's high time we went all in... Time to pull out all the stops... Time to take control, no matter the cost! There ain't no turnin' back from this..! There ain't no turnin' back now!"

For a fleeting moment, tears threatened to spill from his eyes, but he quickly regained his composure, his gaze hardening with resolve.

James stared at his reflection, his gaze growing darker and more determined.

He turned off the faucet, and now he was someone else entirely, someone ready for anything.

"Do it! Or the law's gonna lose two detectives, and the prisons gain a new guest!"

In the dimly lit basement, James descended the stairs, a canister of gasoline clutched tightly in his grip. Bob, bound and battered, pleaded for help through swollen lips, his face a mask of bruises. "Call a damn ambulance! That psychotic partner of yers just knocked a couple a' fillins loose!"

Ignoring Bob's pleas, the young detective began to douse the room with gasoline, his movements deliberate and methodical. He even splashed some of the fuel onto Bob, who seemed to regain some vigor.

"Whoa-whoa-whooooa now! What the hell're you doin'?!"

Bob's protests fell on deaf ears as James continued to saturate their surroundings with fuel.

After finishing spreading the gasoline, the detective tossed aside the canister. The smell of fuel permeated the air, just one spark away from causing Hell to break loose.

"Well, Bob, take a good look at me. I reckon I'm just what you got comin' to ya'!"

James' voice was steely as he confronted Bob, his eyes ablaze with determination.

At that moment, Bob became even more cowardly and pathetic. Big and burly, who knows how many innocents he had tortured and killed. No one would ever know; no one would ever find the bodies, but justice would be served. A blind justice, to be sure, now watched an evil man whimper just because he had been given the same treatment he reserved for his victims. "Please spare me! I got a lotta money! Believe me! It's hidden! I'll take you to it!" Bob's tension broke his speech into fragments, which soon turned into a chant, and then a desperate plea.

"Mighty sorry, Bob, but there are some hurts in our hearts that all the money in the world just can't fix."

With a mere flicker of remorse, James struck a match, the flame casting eerie shadows across the room.

Bob started to scream and thrash in fear.

"Whoa there! Watch out with that! All right, enough jokin' around now!"

His terror was palpable as James held the match aloft, their eyes locked in a chilling standoff.

"Come on, Bob. You didn't think I'd set you on fire for real, did ya'?" With a cruel twist, James extinguished the match.

Bob released the breath he was holding and said, "For a moment there, I thought you were gonna burn me, you ugly son of a bitch! Shit, I'm havin' a heart attack! I need my meds! Ah, call an ambulance, please!"

His relief was short-lived as James' true intentions became clear.

"Hey, Bob... I was messin' with ya!"

"What?" Bob's eyes widened in disbelief.

In one swift motion, James ignited another match and tossed it toward the prisoner, the flames engulfing him in a fiery inferno of screams.

Rain pounded against the car windshield, each drop drowned out by the storm's roar. In the backseat, the little girl slept soundly, unaware of the chaos outside. Kevin's gaze shifted to Bob's house, a dark silhouette against the raging storm. A bolt of lightning illuminated the streets, revealing James sprinting towards the car, his figure blurred by the downpour.

He entered the car and settled into the seat beside the his partner.

"All sorted?" the other detective asked, his voice barely audible over the rain's drumming.

James nodded wearily. "This fire's gonna make forensics scratch their heads," he remarked, resignation in his tone.

"Looks like it's up to us to handle this case in the future," Kevin acknowledged, fatigue creeping into his voice.

"What do we need to report?" James asked.

Kevin paused, pondering his response as he gazed into the storm. "Todd had ties to a Mexican cartel, and Bob was linked to Todd... It'll all be traced through phone records," he began, the weight of their discoveries evident in the new plot. "Todd eliminated his men for control of the drug trade. He killed the woman, because he was a psychopath... and in the end, someone from the cartel dealt with Bob."

"So, Todd's gonna pay for crimes he didn't commit," James mused, resignation coloring his words.

"He's got plenty of other sins he's never answered for... Bob's revelations will haunt me. Todd's ordeal was orchestrated revenge," the detective concluded, burdened by their shared knowledge.

A lightning bolt and thunderclap startled the little girl awake, her frightened whimper filling the car as she reached out to James for comfort. "I'll catch up on the details later. Right now, we need to focus on the girl," James said, his voice gentle yet firm.

Kevin started the engine, the car rumbling to life as they pre-pared to leave the now burning house.

"Where're we takin' her?" Kevin asked, eyes fixed on the road.

"I know people who help Mexican immigrants. They'll take good care of her and might even locate her parents."

"Let's hit the road!" Kevin declared, as they finally drove off.

ALMOST THE END

THE SUNLIGHT STREAMED through the stained-glass windows of St. Joseph's Parish in San Antonio, painting colorful patterns across the empty pews. Father McInney, leaning on his cane, was engaged in conversation with Detective Kevin Sun within the tranquil confines of the parish office. Their voices mingled with the distant hum of the bustling city outside. A strange blend of sadness and newfound serenity hung in the air.

"Detective, I must say, everything you've recounted is truly unbelievable..." Father McInney's voice carried a tone of disbelief and concern.

Seated across from him, the detective listened intently, his gaze fixed on an empty coffee cup resting on the table.

"Unfortunately, it's the unvarnished truth. I've come here to verify. "And you, Father, have just provided me with everything I need for confirmation," the detective replied solemnly, the weight of their past conversation palpable.

Father McInney, his expression troubled, leaned on his cane as he stared out the window, lost in thought. "I remember that night. A man visited Andrew... He threatened him in some way. I informed the authorities, but... but I didn't catch a glimpse of his face. If only I'd had the chance to speak with Andrew," Father McInney recalled, regret seeping into his words.

As their discussion progressed, the detective's thoughts drifted, contemplating the priest's words and the gravity of their implications.

"Were you particularly close to Andrew?" the detective inquired gently, seeking to grasp the depth of their bond.

"He was a good soul. But you could see he bore a heavy burden... and I cared deeply for him. He was like a son to me," Father McInney revealed, his voice tinged with emotion.

Sensing the weight of the moment, the detective rose from his seat, preparing to take his leave.

"The way things are unfoldin', Todd's bound for the death penalty... I just wanna ensure that a certain scoundrel rots in Hell knowin' every last detail," the detective stated firmly, his determination clear.

"In the eyes of the Almighty, there's no harm in bringing the truth to light..." Father McInney mused, torn between his duty and his conscience.

"The decision is yours, and... well, I suppose you have all the time you need to ponder it," the detective acknowledged, tipping his hat respectfully as he headed for the door.

As the detective departed, Father McInney remained deep in thought, his gaze drawn to the crucifix hanging on the wall.

In the quiet confines of the church, the detective's footsteps echoed as he traversed the aisle. Pausing near the exit, he cast a final glance at the crucifix before disappearing into the bustling sounds of the city beyond.

AGAIN... A FEW YEARS LATER

THE HUNTSVILLE UNIT Penitentiary loomed under the unforgiving daylight, its formidable walls casting ominous shadows across the compound. A vehicle approached, navigating through the gates and into the facility.

Father McInney, now in his eighties, emerged from the car clad in priestly attire, his black hat shielding his weathered face from the harsh sun. With the aid of his cane, he made his way towards the prison entrance.

The guards stationed at the gate greeted Father McInney with nods of respect, to which he responded in kind, his steps steady despite his advanced age.

Inside the prison, the priest moved with purpose through the corridors. A prison guard approached him, holding out a stack of papers.

"Howdy, Padre. How're you?" the prison guard greeted him, his voice echoing in the sterile environment.

"I'm getting up there, but I'm praying the good Lord'll keep me around for a little while longer," the holy man replied, his tone infused with humility and faith. The guard chuckled at his response, offering a light-hearted smile in return. Father McInney signed the papers, his movements deliberate yet practiced. "Well, I gotta admit, I use this cane more for style than I do for necessity," the priest jested, eliciting laughter from the guard who gestured for the him to follow, leading him deeper into the penitentiary.

Father McInney was a familiar figure within those walls, especially in recent years. Yet, despite the familiarity, no one noticed that the old priest was unwell, feeling his heart pounding in his chest. He was tense, but he gave his all to pretend that everything was just fine.

A couple of minutes later, Father McInney stepped into an isolation cell, the heavy door shutting behind him with a resounding clang. The room was dimly lit, casting long shadows that seemed to dance with the tension in the air. Todd sat on a metal bed, his hands shackled, his demeanor resigned. "I didn't ask for a priest," the prisoner remarked with a mixture of defiance and bitterness as the holy man approached.

Ignoring Todd's hostility, Father McInney removed his hat and fixed his gaze on the condemned man. "Good morning, Todd," his voice reverberated in the confined space. "I know you didn't ask for spiritual support, but fate has brought me here with you on this day nonetheless."

Todd regarded the priest with skepticism, his expression hardened by years of bitterness and resentment. As Father McInney continued to speak, an intrusive whistle began to pierce the silence, growing louder and more unbearable with each passing moment. "Do you know who I am?" The priest's words were drowned out by the shrill whistle, leaving Todd to decipher his intentions.

"Yeah, the priest might've been a bit full of himself, but he spilled the whole truth right in Todd's face. Todd looked like he was about to snap from

As Todd was dragged through the prison hallways by four police officers, his heart pounded furiously. His cries were muffled by the weight of his anguish. The priest's words echoed in his mind, haunting him with each step. "I knew Andrew, Todd."

Moments later, as if in a twisted nightmare, the death chamber appeared before him, enveloping him entirely.

Todd lay on the bed, held down by guards, his struggles futile against the restraints they put in place. Someone said, "Cut it out, Todd! Quit squirming or we'll pin you down! You know one way or another, this has to be done!"

The old priest's words kept echoing in Todd's mind as if they were being repeated for every single second of his life—a chant he had never really noticed before. What confusion. What searing rage. The prisoner was overtaken by utter madness, fueled by his complete helplessness. The guards restrained him and started to sedate him.

"You ruined his life and that of his friend Daly, whom he loved deeply." Todd's mind was in turmoil, flooded with images of Andrew, tears streaming down his face, standing on the church tower's ledge, his gaze fixed on the nocturnal skyline as he wrestled with his inner demons. "Andrew tried to move forward, to start anew, but you came back to him like the devil himself." Andrew braced himself to leap into the abyss, only to… stop abruptly. "Terry Brooke was there to kill him first, and that's exactly what she did… saving him… as he became her."

Signed: A priest who confessed to a priest.